Current
CONTROVERSIES

America's Role in a
Changing World

D1566257

Other Books in the Current Controversies Series

America's Role in a Changing World

Eamon Doyle, Book Editor

GREENHAVEN PUBLISHING

Published in 2023 by Greenhaven Publishing, LLC
29 E. 21st Street
New York, NY 10010

Articles in Greenhaven Publishing anthologies are often edited for length to meet page
requirements. In addition, original titles of these works are changed to clearly present
the main thesis and to explicitly indicate the author's opinion. Every effort is made to
ensure that Greenhaven Publishing accurately reflects the original intent of the authors.
Every effort has been made to trace the owners of the copyrighted material.

Cover image: Gil C/Shutterstock.com

Library of Congress Cataloging-in-Publication Data

Names: Doyle, Eamon, 1988– editor.
Title: America's role in a changing world / Eamon Doyle, book editor.
Description: First edition. | New York : Greenhaven Publishing, 2023. |
   Series: Current controversies. | Includes bibliographical references and
   index. | Audience: Ages 15 | Audience: Grades 10–12 | Summary:
   "Anthology of curated essays exploring changes in the United States, its
   global allies and adversaries, and their relationships, in recent
   years"— Provided by publisher.
Identifiers: LCCN 2021062231 | ISBN 9781534508897 (library binding) | ISBN
   9781534508880 (paperback) | ISBN 9781534508903 (ebook)
Subjects: LCSH: World politics—21st century—Juvenile literature. | United
   States—Foreign relations—21st century—Juvenile literature. | United
   States—Politics and government—21st century—Juvenile literature.
Classification: LCC E895 .A442 2023 | DDC 327.73009/05—dc23/eng/20220201
LC record available at https://lccn.loc.gov/2021062231

Manufactured in the United States of America

Website: http://greenhavenpublishing.com

Contents

these risks, the ultimate consequences of the withdrawal are still undetermined and will depend largely on US policy in the region in the years ahead.

Yes: Failure to achieve a stable victory in Afghanistan and the chaos of the withdrawal has undermined US credibility and contributed to perceptions that its power is in decline.

Lt. Gen. Richard P. Mills and Erielle Davidson

The authors emphasize the risks associated with the US withdrawal from Afghanistan and analyze how those risks are likely to impact US-Chinese competition. Beijing could leverage its relationship with the Taliban to gain access and possibly control over Afghan natural resources.

Matthew Kroenig and Jeffrey Cimmino

Characterizing the withdrawal as a betrayal of repeated assurances that US policymakers offered the Afghan people during the occupation, the authors question whether international actors will be able to trust American commitments in the future.

No: Despite the failures of the American occupation of Afghanistan, the withdrawal is unlikely to permanently diminish US global influence.

Vanda Felbab-Brown

The author argues in favor of the Biden administration's decision to end the occupation of Afghanistan and withdraw all military forces from the country. In her assessment, the withdrawal represents a wise reorientation of US national security policy in the Middle East.

Anthony H. Cordesman

The author urges Americans to adopt a broad historical view of the US presence in Afghanistan and to focus less on the withdrawal and more on the larger story of the war and the nearly twenty-year occupation.

Chapter 3: Is the US Prepared to Contend with Hybrid Warfare Tactics Increasingly Favored by Its Enemies?

economic coercion. Because of the enormous risk in this area, the authors argue that energy security must be a top priority for Western defense and security officials.

David R. Shedd and Ivana Stradner

Vladimir Putin is conducting a hybrid war against the United States, largely succeeding in his goal of destabilizing American politics and society. US intelligence and defense officials have too often examined the Russian campaign through the lens of traditional warfare and must shift their strategic mindset to contend with the Kremlin's hybrid campaign on its own terms.

Chapter 4: Has Recent Political Turmoil Undermined the US Position as the World's Leading Democracy?

Daniel I. Weiner and Tim Lau

Institutional probity and procedural norms represent the foundation of political legitimacy in a liberal democratic state, and President Trump's behavior following the election has had a corrosive effect on the body politic in America.

Yes: Recent dysfunction in US politics has dramatically diminished America's credibility in advocating for liberal democratic norms around the world.

Jon Bateman

Since the end of the Second World War, US national security has focused almost exclusively on threats associated with foreign actors. But our contemporary political dysfunction has metastasized into a full-blown national security risk, which will require security officials to adjust and reframe the purview of their work.

Sandra Feder

An interview with Terry Moe and William Howell offers a stark and sobering analysis of the problems currently facing the American democratic system and identifies a number of structural conditions within the system itself that are contributing to the overall political dysfunction and that, importantly, will be very difficult to address with top-down reform measures.

No: The US remains the world's most powerful democracy and is fully capable of advocating for liberal democratic values on the international stage.

Elaine Kamarck

Kamarck examines the ongoing debate among American political analysts about the impact of President Trump's term in office, arguing that, for the most part, the formal institutions of American democracy held firm against the various pressures exerted by Trump and his supporters (particularly in the aftermath of the 2020 election, when Trump refused to concede defeat).

Kelly Magsamen, Max Bergmann, Michael Fuchs, and Trevor Sutton

The authors recommend strategies that US foreign policy officials could adopt in order to strengthen America's role as the world's leading democracy in the face of challenges both at home and abroad. In spite of the current global surge of populism and authoritarianism, America remains in a strong position to exercise leadership among the global community of democratic nations.

Foreword

"Controversy" is a word that has an undeniably unpleasant connotation. It carries a definite negative charge. Controversy can spoil family gatherings, spread a chill around classroom and campus discussion, inflame public discourse, open raw civic wounds, and lead to the ouster of public officials. We often feel that controversy is almost akin to bad manners, a rude and shocking eruption of that which must not be spoken or thought of in polite, tightly guarded society. To avoid controversy, to quell controversy, is often seen as a public good, a victory for etiquette, perhaps even a moral or ethical imperative.

Yet the studious, deliberate avoidance of controversy is also a whitewashing, a denial, a death threat to democracy. It is a false sterilizing and sanitizing and superficial ordering of the messy, ragged, chaotic, at times ugly processes by which a healthy democracy identifies and confronts challenges, engages in passionate debate about appropriate approaches and solutions, and arrives at something like a consensus and a broadly accepted and supported way forward. Controversy is the megaphone, the speaker's corner, the public square through which the citizenry finds and uses its voice. Controversy is the life's blood of our democracy and absolutely essential to the vibrant health of our society.

Our present age is certainly no stranger to controversy. We are consumed by fierce debates about technology, privacy, political correctness, poverty, violence, crime and policing, guns, immigration, civil and human rights, terrorism, militarism, environmental protection, and gender and racial equality. Loudly competing voices are raised every day, shouting opposing opinions, putting forth competing agendas, and summoning starkly different visions of a utopian or dystopian future. Often these voices attempt to shout the others down; there is precious little listening and considering among the cacophonous din. Yet listening and considering, too, are essential to the health of a democracy. If controversy is democracy's lusty lifeblood, respectful listening and careful thought are its higher faculties, its brain, its conscience.

Current Controversies does not shy away from or attempt to hush the loudly competing voices. It seeks to provide readers with as wide and representative as possible a range of articulate voices on any given controversy of the day, separates each one out to allow it to be heard clearly and fairly, and encourages careful listening to each of these well-crafted, thoughtfully expressed opinions, supplied by some of today's leading academics, thinkers, analysts, politicians, policy makers, economists, activists, change agents, and advocates. Only after listening to a wide range of opinions on an issue, evaluating the strengths and weaknesses of each argument, assessing how well the facts and available evidence mesh with the stated opinions and conclusions, and thoughtfully and critically examining one's own beliefs and conscience can the reader begin to arrive at his or her own conclusions and articulate his or her own stance on the spotlighted controversy.

This process is facilitated and supported in each Current Controversies volume by an introduction and chapter overviews that provide readers with the essential context they need to begin engaging with the spotlighted controversies, with the debates surrounding them, and with their own perhaps shifting or nascent opinions on them. Chapters are organized around several key questions that are answered with diverse opinions representing all points on the political spectrum. In its content, organization, and methodology, readers are encouraged to determine the authors' point of view and purpose, interrogate and analyze the various arguments and their rhetoric and structure, evaluate the arguments' strengths and weaknesses, test their claims against available facts and evidence, judge the validity of the reasoning, and bring into clearer, sharper focus the reader's own beliefs and conclusions and how they may differ from or align with those in the collection or those of classmates.

Research has shown that reading comprehension skills improve dramatically when students are provided with compelling, intriguing, and relevant "discussable" texts. The subject matter of these collections could not be more compelling, intriguing, or urgently relevant to today's students and the world they are poised to inherit. The anthologized articles also provide the basis for stimulating, lively, and passionate classroom debates. Students who are compelled to anticipate objections to their own argument and identify the flaws in those of an opponent read more carefully, think more critically, and steep themselves in relevant context, facts, and information more thoroughly. In short, using discussable text of the kind provided by every single volume in the Current Controversies series encourages close reading, facilitates reading comprehension, fosters research, strengthens critical thinking, and greatly enlivens and energizes classroom discussion and participation. The entire learning process is deepened, extended, and strengthened.

If we are to foster a knowledgeable, responsible, active, and engaged citizenry, we must provide readers with the intellectual, interpretive, and critical-thinking tools and experience necessary to make sense of the world around them and of the all-important debates and arguments that inform it. We must encourage them not to run away from or attempt to quell controversy but to embrace it in a responsible, conscientious, and thoughtful way, to sharpen and strengthen their own informed opinions by listening to and critically analyzing those of others. This series encourages respectful engagement with and analysis of current controversies and competing opinions and fosters a resulting increase in the strength and rigor of one's own opinions and stances. As such, it helps readers assume their rightful place in the public square and provides them with the skills necessary to uphold their awesome responsibility—guaranteeing the continued and future health of a vital, vibrant, and free democracy.

Introduction

> *"For more than 70 years, the United States' ability to do good in the world and secure its international interests has been inseparable from its commitment to democracy at home and abroad."*[1]

Throughout most of the late twentieth century, the United States played a unique and central role in the international community. As the world's most powerful and influential democracy, the US exercised leadership in several ways: (1) by promoting liberal and free market values around the world; (2) by resisting Soviet expansionism during the Cold War (1947–1989); and (3) by helping to create a body of international norms and institutions (e.g., NATO, the UN) to encourage cooperative diplomacy and prevent the outbreak of a third world war. As the Cold War came to an end and the Soviet Union collapsed, it seemed to many as though the United States stood alone atop the world order as the last remaining global superpower. Historians often refer to this period as the "unipolar moment." It was a heady time in American culture. Some analysts speculated that the end of the Cold War signaled a dialectical turning point in world history, one that would open the door to a new era of liberal hegemony. (The most prominent example of this argument can be found in Francis Fukuyama's 1992 book *The End of History*.) But events would quickly prove such theories premature, if not outright mistaken.

The 9/11 terrorist attacks in 2001 shattered Americans' sense of domestic security. Subsequent wars in Iraq and Afghanistan undermined perceptions of American military strength and diplomatic acumen. The 2008 financial crisis led to troubling questions about the United States' ability to manage the liberal international order that it had played such a key role in shaping. At the same time, technology was upending nearly every aspect of daily life around the world, and the rapid development and quasi-liberalization of the Chinese economy was shifting the balance of global power.

By the end of the 2000s, it seemed clear that the unipolar moment was over, and observers began a series of debates about the future of American power and influence around the world. *Current Controversies: America's Role in a Changing World* takes a close look at four key topics that have shaped these debates: the rise of China as a global superpower, the proliferation of hybrid warfare, the failure of American-led wars in the Middle East, and the future of democracy around the world.

Among the challenges currently facing American foreign policy officials, few have proved as complex and vexing as managing the rise of China. US-Chinese competition represents the most significant instance of great power conflict since the Cold War, and in some areas China appears to have the advantage. Foreign policy analysts Aynne Kokas and Oriana Skylar Mastro offer the following appraisal:

> The Chinese government is having a propaganda field day. More than ever, the US looks like a country in decline, discouraging to allies and potential partners. Chinese commentators have noted that America's days as the "city on the hill" have come to an end. [...] Initiatives such as the Digital Silk Road, a program to build out global digital infrastructure using Chinese technology, and the Health Silk Road, a plan to export Chinese health expertise through things such as COVID-19 laboratories and vaccine diplomacy, draw on China's comparative advantage in a top-down soft power approach.[2]

But while China may represent the most formidable adversary the US has faced since the end of the Cold War, a number of other actors are also challenging American leadership on the world stage.

States like Russia, Turkey, Iran, and North Korea are increasingly utilizing asymmetric and hybrid warfare tactics to disrupt American foreign policy initiatives. The proliferation of such methods has altered the landscape of global competition in a number of ways. Security analysts Michael Rühle and Clare Roberts write:

> Today's security environment is increasingly complex. The times when peace, crisis and conflict were three distinct phases, when conflicts were fought largely with military means, and when adversaries were well known, are over. Cyberattacks are hitting nations below the threshold of a military attack. Social media campaigns create alternative realities that seek to destabilize political communities without a single soldier crossing a single border. And the "hybrid" combination of military and non-military instruments creates ambiguities that make NATO's situational awareness and, consequently, consensual and speedy decision-making far more difficult.[3]

The fact that this new landscape of hybrid competition has emerged in the wake of perceived US military failures in the Middle East creates further challenges.

But despite the daunting scale and complexity of challenges facing American officials, some observers remain optimistic about the United States' capacity for global leadership and the future of democracy around the world. In a recent report, Center for American Progress analysts Kelly Magsamen, Max Bergmann, Michael Fuchs, and Trevor Sutton offer the following assessment:

> For more than 70 years, the United States' ability to do good in the world and secure its international interests has been inseparable from its commitment to democracy at home and abroad. [...] The global system of democratic alliances, institutions, and norms the United States helped create and lead after World War II has improved material conditions and brought peace and prosperity to hundreds of millions of people across the world. Bolstering that democratic system and the democratic values that underpin it will ensure that

future generations can also enjoy the fruits of democracy and a liberal world.[4]

The world is changing quickly, and the global environment is likely to remain dynamic and unpredictable for many years to come. But it is also clear that America's role in that environment will be highly consequential. The United States may no longer occupy the position of global predominance that it enjoyed during the unipolar moment, but its influence is still robust and its future as a global leader will depend on the strategic acumen and decision-making skills of its top leadership over the next several years.

Notes

1. "Securing a Democratic World," by Kelly Magsamen, Max Bergmann, Michael Fuchs, and Trevor Sutton, Center for American Progress, September 5, 2018.

2. "The Soft War That America Is Losing," by Aynne Kokas and Oriana Skylar Mastro, *The Australian Financial Review*, January 15, 2021.

3. "Enlarging NATO's Toolbox to Counter Hybrid Threats," by Michael Rühle and Clare Roberts, *NATO Review*, March 19, 2021.

4. "Securing a Democratic World," by Kelly Magsamen, Max Bergmann, Michael Fuchs, and Trevor Sutton, Center for American Progress, September 5, 2018.

Is China Positioned to Become the Dominant Global Power in the Twenty-First Century?

Overview: International Perceptions of US-Chinese Strategic Competition

Laura Silver, Kat Devlin, and Christine Huang

Laura Silver is an expert on international public opinion research and a senior researcher at Pew Research Center. Kat Devlin is a former researcher at Pew Research Center's Global Attitudes Project. Christine Huang is a research associate at Pew Research Center.

The United States is named as the top economic power in 21 of the 34 countries surveyed, while China is considered the top economy in 12 (the U.S. and China are tied as top economic power in Lebanon). Still, publics are relatively divided, as no more than half name either country as the top economy in most countries. And few consider Japan or the countries of the European Union as the leading economic power.

Generally, most non-European countries see the United States as the world's leading economic power, while those in Europe tend to name China. For example, in the Asia-Pacific countries surveyed, a median of 46% say the U.S. is the top economy, while a 25% median say the same about China. Across many of these countries, too, there is little ambiguity about which country is dominant, with double-digit differences between the shares who choose the U.S. and who choose China as the top economy. This is most extreme in South Korea, where there is a 70 percentage point difference between those who cite American economic supremacy (82%) and Chinese dominance (12%). South Koreans are also more likely to name the U.S. as the world's leading economy this year compared with last year (up 15 percentage points). Within the region, Indonesians and Australians stand out for being more likely to choose China as the leading global economy, though

Indonesians are somewhat divided (21% U.S., 24% China) and about as many of them name Japan (22%) as the leading economy.

Across the Middle East and North Africa, majorities or pluralities consider the U.S. to be the world's leading economy. In Israel, six-in-ten hold this view, and about half say the same in Turkey and Tunisia (49% and 47%, respectively). The U.S. and China are tied in Lebanon, with a third naming each as the top economy. In Tunisia and Israel, the belief that the U.S. is the dominant economic power grew by double digits from 2018 (up 12 and 10 points, respectively).

Likewise, more see the U.S. than China as the top economy in all three sub-Saharan African countries surveyed, though the publics are largely divided. In Nigeria and South Africa, the tendency to name the U.S. is a departure from last year, when more in both countries named China as the world's top economic power.

The U.S. remains the top choice for all three Latin American countries surveyed. However, roughly a third still name China as the top economy in Mexico and Argentina, and this share has gone up by 6 percentage points in Argentina since 2018.

Only in Europe do more countries name China as the world's leading economy. A median of 41% across the 14 EU member nations surveyed name China, compared with a median of 39% who say the same about the United States. China's lead over the U.S. is especially clear in Germany, the Netherlands, the Czech Republic and France, where people are at least 10 percentage points more likely to see China as the leading economy. In France, the share that views China as the top economic power has increased by 7 percentage points since 2018, flipping the top choice from the U.S. to China. Spaniards, Swedes and Bulgarians are more muted, with about 5-point differences in their evaluations of the two economies. Those in the UK are about equally likely to point to China or the U.S. as the top economy (42% vs. 41%). In five European countries that have consistently been asked which economy is strongest over the past decade—

France, Germany, Spain, the UK and Poland—China has come out on top more often than not.

Still, Lithuanians are 23 percentage points more likely to see the U.S. as the top economy. Poles and Slovaks are also at least 10 points more likely to choose the U.S. over China. Greeks, Italians, and Hungarians similarly evaluate the U.S. economy as more powerful than the Chinese economy, but by a slimmer margin (5 points in all three countries).

Opinions in Russia and Ukraine are divided. Ukrainians say the U.S. is dominant by a margin of 22 points, while Russians choose China by 33 points. For Russians, this is a 14-point increase in the share who chose China in 2018, and a continuation of a steady upward trend in the share that see China as the world's leading economy.

Majorities in Most Countries See Both U.S. and China Heavily Influencing Their Domestic Economies

Majorities in most countries surveyed say China has a substantial amount of influence on the economic affairs of their countries. Across the 16 nations asked, a median of 63% say China has a great deal or fair amount of influence.

In the Asia-Pacific countries surveyed, South Koreans, Japanese and Australians are especially likely to say China has a great deal or fair amount of influence on their country's economy, with about nine-in-ten or more holding this opinion. Lebanon also stands out in the Middle East, as 85% say China has at least a fair amount of influence on Lebanese economic conditions.

Roughly three-quarters in Kenya and Nigeria say the same, while about six-in-ten see at least a fair amount of Chinese influence on their domestic economies in the three Latin American countries surveyed.

Across these same 16 countries, a median of 75% say the U.S. has a great deal or fair amount of influence on economic conditions in their country, compared with a median of 19% who say it has little or no influence.

Perceived influence is highest in South Korea (96%), Japan (94%) and Israel (88%), and lowest in Indonesia—the only country where fewer than half (45%) say the U.S. plays a large role in their economic affairs.

When comparing the two superpowers, by a slim margin, more people in the Asia-Pacific region say China plays a large role in their country's economic conditions (six-country median of 78%) than say the same of the U.S. (74%). But in South Korea and Japan, upwards of nine-in-ten say both superpowers have a great deal of influence. Indians and Filipinos are about 10 percentage points more likely to see American influence on their economies, while those in Australia are 18 points more likely to see China's muscle.

All three sub-Saharan African publics surveyed are more likely to see Chinese economic influence, with about a 10-point difference in Nigeria and South Africa. Conversely, those in Latin America are more likely to see influence from the U.S.

And, in the Middle East and North Africa, those in Israel and Turkey are more likely to identify influence from the U.S., with a difference of about 20 points or more. Those in Lebanon and Tunisia are about as likely to say the U.S. or China have a great deal or fair amount of influence.

More Describe Chinese Influence on Economy as Positive Than Say the Same of U.S. Influence

People who said that China or the U.S. had at least some influence on economic conditions of their country were also asked to rate that influence as either positive of negative.

In Asia-Pacific countries, evaluations of Chinese influence are fairly divided; Australians, Filipinos and Indonesians are more likely to see Chinese influence as positive than negative, while Japanese, South Koreans and Indians identify Chinese influence as more negative than positive.

Opinions in the Middle East and North Africa are also conflicted. Those in Israel and Lebanon are much more likely to see the Chinese impact on economic conditions in their country as positive. Tunisians also see Chinese influence as more positive than negative, but by a smaller margin. Turks more frequently see Chinese influence negatively.

Opinions elsewhere are more clear-cut. Majorities in the sub-Saharan African countries surveyed say Chinese influence is positive, especially in Nigeria, where about seven-in-ten hold this opinion. About four-in-ten or more see Chinese influence positively in the Latin American nations surveyed as well.

Substantial minorities in most countries did not offer any opinion of China's influence.

When it comes to American influence, evaluations are somewhat less positive; a median of 42% rate it positively, while 34% say the U.S. is having more of a negative influence on economic conditions in their country.

Those in the Asia-Pacific region are more likely than not to describe U.S. economic influence in their country in positive terms. This is most true in the Philippines, where 65% say the U.S. is having a positive influence on their economic conditions and 25% say the U.S. is having a negative influence—a difference of 40 percentage points. Indians, Indonesians and South Koreans are also much more likely to see the U.S. influence as positive than negative. Only in Australia do more say the U.S. has a negative influence (46%) than a positive one (38%). Japanese are relatively divided on the issue, with 42% citing positive influence and 39% negative.

Across the Middle East and North African countries surveyed, most publics are more likely to see U.S. economic influence unfavorably, even as Israelis almost uniformly describe America's role as good (82% positive). In Turkey especially, about three-quarters say the U.S. has a negative influence on their domestic economic conditions. Those in Lebanon and Tunisia are at least 20 points more likely to see the influence as negative.

More in the three sub-Saharan countries surveyed say the U.S. has a positive economic influence than say it has a negative influence. Still, substantial minorities of around one-in-five or more describe it negatively. And opinion is mixed in the three Latin American countries surveyed, with Brazilians largely describing the American role favorably (44%) and Argentines and Mexicans saying the opposite (55% and 46% negative, respectively).

When directly comparing the perceived positive influence from the U.S. and China, outside of the Asia-Pacific region, Chinese economic influence is largely seen in more positive terms than American influence. For example, across three of the Middle East and North African countries surveyed, people are substantially more likely to describe China's role in their economy in positive terms than they are America's role. In Lebanon, about twice as many say China is having a good influence (50%) than say the same of the U.S. (26%). Most in sub-Saharan Africa and Latin America, too, describe Chinese influence positively, even as substantial numbers in most countries also see U.S. influence positively.

But, in much of the Asia-Pacific region, people are more likely to evaluate the U.S. economic influence positively than the Chinese, or at least to see them comparably. Only in Australia and Indonesia do more say China's influence is good than say the same about the U.S. But, in Indonesia, China's influence is seen more positively by a very thin margin.

Favorable views of Chinese economic influence are more common among those who think their country has good economic ties with China and those who prefer a close economic relationship to China. Those who feel similarly toward the U.S. are also more likely to see U.S. economic influence as good.

Most Say Current Economic Relations with Both China and U.S. Are Good

When it comes to the current state of economic relations with China, publics are much more likely to describe them as good (median of 66%) than bad (21%). Outside of Canada, the U.S. and some of the Asia-Pacific countries surveyed, around half or more in every other country see current economic ties positively.

In the wake of major trade disputes and political tensions with China, around half in both the U.S. and Canada describe current bilateral economic relations as poor. In South Korea and Japan, too, 66% and 51%, respectively, say relations are negative.

In the Middle East and North Africa, majorities in all except Turkey say the economic relationship between their country and China is going well. Even in Turkey, about half say the relationship is positive.

Likewise, majorities in the sub-Saharan African and Latin American countries surveyed also rate their economic relationship with China positively.

Most also say current economic relations with the United States are going well; a median of 64% say relations are in good shape, compared with 23% who say the opposite.

This sense is highest among Israelis, 96% of whom say American-Israeli economic ties are positive. The other Middle East and North African countries surveyed are the only countries where fewer than half say relations are currently positive. This is especially true in Turkey, where about two-thirds said economic ties between their country and the U.S. were bad, even before the U.S. imposed new sanctions on Turkey in October.

Across the Asia-Pacific region, six-in-ten or more in each country say their economic ties to the U.S. are currently good. Around three-quarters or more take this position in India (74%), Australia (85%) and the Philippines (89%).

Attitudes in the sub-Saharan African countries surveyed are also positive, with roughly seven-in-ten or more in each country saying relations are positive. Opinions in the Latin American countries surveyed are similar, though less effusive; fewer than two-thirds in all three countries say their economic ties with the U.S. are positive, and substantial minorities say the ties are bad.

Canadians also have tempered evaluations, with about two-thirds saying that ties are good and about a third disagreeing.

And, when comparing economic ties to the U.S. and to China, many publics have a sanguine view of their current economic relationship with both superpowers. More than two-thirds in each of the sub-Saharan African countries surveyed describe current economic ties with both China and the U.S. as good, and around half or more say the same in each of the Latin American countries surveyed.

In the Asia-Pacific region, ties with the U.S. are more frequently rated as good in India, South Korea and Japan. Majorities in those countries see economic relations with the U.S. positively, while only minorities say the same of China. The difference is especially pronounced in India, where nearly three-quarters say they have a good economic relationship with the U.S. and about four-in-ten say the same about China, a difference of 35 percentage points.

This pattern is reversed in the Middle East and North Africa, where all publics but Israel rate their economic relationships with China more positively. This is especially true in Lebanon, where there is a 40-point difference between the share who say their ties with the U.S. are good and the share who say ties with China are good. Only in Israel do more say ties to the U.S. are good, and even there, eight-in-ten still see their economic ties with China positively.

Stronger Economic Ties to U.S. Preferred

Sixteen publics were asked whether they prefer stronger economic ties with the U.S. or China. On balance, more prefer for their country to have closer relations with the U.S. (a median of 46%) than China (32%). Opinions are unified in the Asia-Pacific countries surveyed, with greater shares in all six preferring strong U.S. economic ties. Those in Japan, South Korea, the Philippines and India especially prefer ties with the U.S.; they are more likely to choose relations with the U.S. over China by about 40 percentage points or more. For Australians and South Koreans, this year's results are a reversal from opinions in 2015, when more preferred strong economic ties with China.

For the four Middle East and North African countries surveyed, opinions are mixed. Those in Turkey and Israel say strong ties with the U.S. are more important, and those in Lebanon and Tunisia say close economic ties with China are more important. Still, substantial minorities in Lebanon and Israel volunteer that strong ties with both are more important, and about two-thirds in Tunisia say the same.

In the sub-Saharan African countries surveyed, only those in Nigeria would rather have strong economic ties with China than with the U.S. About three-in-ten in Nigeria also volunteer that strong ties with both are more important. Argentines are the only public of the three Latin American countries surveyed that chooses ties with China over ties with the U.S., though by only a 2-point margin.

Preferences for strong economic ties with the U.S. or China differ based on perceptions of economic power. Those who say China is the world's leading economic power are more likely to prefer strong economic ties with China, and vice versa. In Lebanon, for example, those who say China is the world's leading economic power are 62 percentage points more likely than those who think the U.S. is the top economy to want strong economic ties with China.

Likewise, those with favorable views of China are more likely to choose strong economic ties with China in most countries. Favorable views of Chinese investment and China's growing military power are also tied to a preference for ties with China.

A New Generation of Chinese Are Embracing Change and Innovation

Zak Dychtwald

Zak Dychtwald is founder of the market insights firm Young China Group and author of Young China: How the Restless Generation Will Change Their Country and the World *(St. Regis Press, 2018). He has delivered lectures on Chinese culture at the Aspen Ideas Festival and the Wall Street Journal CEO Summit.*

The future of the Chinese economy lies in innovation, and everyone in China knows it. But that hasn't always been true. Innovation didn't drive the manufacturing miracle that has unfolded in China over the past half century, during which some 700 million people have been raised—or lifted themselves—out of desperate poverty. Instead the driver has in large part been what might be called brute-force imitation. Relying on a seemingly limitless supply of cheap labor, provided by the hundreds of millions of ambitious workers born during the postwar baby boom, China devoted itself prodigiously to the production of other countries' innovations. The effort enabled a country that missed the Industrial Revolution to absorb the world's most modern manufacturing advances in just a decade or two. Fittingly, China earned a reputation as a global copycat.

Now times are changing. China's Baby Boomers are being replaced by its Millennials, born under the country's one-child policy, which was officially launched in 1979 and designed to get birth rates below replacement level. It worked—but it also created a new demographic reality: China today doesn't have enough people in its rising Millennial and Gen Z workforce to replenish the ranks of its disappearing Baby Boomers. According to its National Bureau of Statistics, China will have 81 million

"China's New Innovation Advantage," by Zak Dychtwald, *Harvard Business Review*, May–June 2021. Reprinted by permission.

fewer working-age people in 2030 than in 2015; after 2030 that
population is projected to decline by an average of 7.6 million
annually. This has profound implications. With its pool of younger
workers shrinking, China can no longer rely on imitation if it
hopes to grow and support its aging population. It will have to
rely on innovation instead.

But can China innovate? Can it compete at a global level with
developed nations that have built their economies on innovation
for decades? Many observers are doubtful. In recent years, they
note, the West has steadily produced an abundance of innovations
and innovators, while China has produced relatively few. In March
2014 this magazine published "Why China Can't Innovate," by
Regina M. Abrami, William C. Kirby, and F. Warren McFarlan,
an article that captured the conventional wisdom. The authors'
arguments were sound and well supported at the time. But just
two years later eight of the 10 companies that had reached a
$1 billion valuation in the shortest time ever were Chinese—and
six of those eight were founded the year that article was published.

Those are startling numbers for a country that in 2020 ranked
only 14th on the Global Innovation Index. Something clearly
propelled those Chinese companies to the top, but the metrics
we use to evaluate innovation have missed it. We tend to focus on
people and companies that generate big new ideas—charismatic
heroes with dash, daring, and dynamic thinking. By that measure
the U.S. innovation ecosystem stands apart. But in the past five
years, as an "innovation cold war" has taken shape between world
powers, China has achieved a kind of parity with the United
States—and the driving force behind its success may not be its
innovators at all.

To understand what's powering the global rise of Chinese
companies, we need to recognize that China now has at its
disposal a resource that no other country has: a vast population
that has lived through unprecedented amounts of change and,
consequently, has developed an astonishing propensity for

adopting and adapting to innovations, at a speed and scale that is unmatched elsewhere on earth.

It's that aspect of China's innovation ecosystem—its hundreds of millions of hyper-adoptive and hyper-adaptive consumers—that makes China so globally competitive today. In the end, innovations must be judged by people's willingness to use them. And on that front China has no peer.

[...]

Closing the Innovation Gap

To compete successfully with China in the decades ahead, countries and companies will need to start strategically prioritizing not just innovation input, in the form of heroically imagined new tools and technologies, but also innovation output that becomes transformational through rapid adoption on a very large scale. In the short term, China has a clear advantage in terms of output, thanks to its huge population of hyper-adopters and hyper-adapters, and as a result it is poised to take the lead in the innovation arms race. But if business leaders outside China take the following steps, they can begin to close the gap.

Pay Attention

As the science-fiction writer William Gibson once wrote, "The future is already here—it's just not evenly distributed." That's an insight worth applying to China, which in some cases is years ahead of global markets and so provides an excellent way of peering into the future, particularly when it comes to digital and retail trends.

Consider Visa, Mastercard, and other key global players in noncash payments, which to date have resisted encouraging mobile payment, ostensibly unwilling to fully disrupt their credit card empires. If China is any guide, those companies could be headed for a "Kodak moment," as when Kodak, in response to the emergence of the digital camera, read the future wrong and made the disastrous decision to define itself as a film rather than a photo company. What's in store globally is probably a lot like what we already see in China, where people trust platforms like AliPay and WeChat Pay for all things financial, from purchases to loans to investments. But the big credit card companies still have an opportunity to pioneer and encourage mobile payment globally rather than ceding the market to tech giants, as the banks in China have largely done.

Similarly, the online and offline retail ecosystems in China are merging in ways that are years ahead of what's happening in the United States. In Chinese grocery and convenience stores, it is now commonplace to see rows of QR codes below meat and produce. Scanning a QR code with a smartphone will reveal the product's entire story, from, say, where a cut of salmon was sourced to how far it was shipped. Similarly, scanning a tech product in a store can bring up the brand video and user ratings. This is what Alibaba calls New Retail, and it could well become the global norm, because it allows brands to deepen their relationships with customers directly. Nearly all multinationals operating in China have adopted this sort of digital-first, China-forward strategy. (U.S. companies operating there have rolled out far more advanced versions of this strategy than the ones they currently use at home.)

The lesson here is that Chinese consumers have come to expect such a rich online brand experience. Failing to provide it, or being seen as having fallen behind, will doom a company in the market. The Chinese can show companies looking to gain competitive advantage in U.S. markets how to develop better touch points with consumers.

Up Your Imitation Game
If you're used to believing in your own exceptionalism, leaning into imitation as a strategy can feel like a declaration of defeat. But innovation has always been about both invention and imitation. We don't think less of Apple because Steve Jobs got the idea for the mouse from Xerox. Genius steals, and it always has. To

compete with China, imitation must be a weapon in the arsenal of global companies—one they're willing to use.

Some of the smartest non-Chinese companies already understand this and are looking to Chinese rivals for ideas. That's what Facebook did in 2019 when it added an integrated payment option to its chat function, five years after WeChat had introduced a similar option on a mass scale, in a pioneering example of how to productively fuse the worlds of social and commercial technology. It's what Amazon did when it modeled its Prime Day (a wildly successful annual event during which Prime members receive all sorts of sale offers and discounts) on Alibaba's Singles Day. Instagram got the idea for its Reels feature from TikTok. The list goes on and on.

Companies looking to China for ideas should consider these courses of action:

Lead from your China team. We've all been told to localize for China. Take that a step further and, at least in part, lead from China. Few companies empower their China teams to help create global strategy. That's a missed opportunity. What is second nature to your China team may be revelatory to your other teams. What you learn about local strategy in China may well help transform your global strategy.

Expose your best. Send your best and brightest to China. Expose them to new ideas there. Expand their sense of what's possible. I have spoken with delegations representing a range of companies, from German auto manufacturers to U.S. retailers, who told me that part of their mission in visiting China was to learn from the digital ecosystem there and take those lessons back home.

Stay informed at China speed. As the saying goes, "If you haven't been to China in the past six months, you haven't been to today's China." Stay informed constantly and consciously. Quarterly updates from trendspotters and on-the-ground resources are a good start. For global executives, video updates illustrating trends and experiences can be a close second to travel.

The Chinese Approach to Climate and Environmental Reform Is Working

Kelly Sims Gallagher and Fang Zhang

Kelly Sims Gallagher is academic dean and professor of energy and environmental policy at the Fletcher School at Tufts University. She previously served as senior China adviser in the Special Envoy for Climate Change at the US State Department. Fang Zhang is associate professor in the School of Environment at Tsinghua University in Beijing.

As the effects of climate change become more widespread and alarming, U.N. Secretary-General António Guterres has called on nations to step up their plans for cutting greenhouse gas emissions. Every country has a part to play, but if the world's largest emitters fail to meet their commitments, the goal of holding global warming to a manageable level will remain out of reach.

U.S. carbon dioxide emissions are on the rise after several years of decline, due in part to the Trump administration's repeal or delay of Obama administration policies. In contrast, China—the world largest emitter—appears to be honoring its climate targets under the 2015 Paris Agreement, as we documented in a recent article with colleagues.

We study many aspects of China's energy and climate policy, including industrial energy efficiency and reforestation. Our analysis indicates that if China fully executes existing policies and finishes reforming its electric power sector into a market-based system, its carbon dioxide emissions are likely to peak well before its 2030 target.

"China Is Positioned to Lead on Climate Change as the US Rolls Back Its Policies," by Kelly Sims Gallagher and Fang Zhang, The Conversation, September 12, 2019. https://theconversation.com/china-is-positioned-to-lead-on-climate-change-as-the-us-rolls-back-its-policies-114897. Licensed under CC BY-ND-4.0 International.

China's Climate Portfolio

Over the last decade China has positioned itself as a global leader on climate action through aggressive investments and a bold mix of climate, renewable energy, energy efficiency and economic policies. As one of us (Kelly Sims Gallagher) documents in the recent book *Titans of the Climate*, China has implemented more than 100 policies related to lowering its energy use and greenhouse gas emissions.

Notable examples include a feed-in-tariff policy for renewable energy generators, which offers them a guaranteed price for their power; energy efficiency standards for power plants, motor vehicles, buildings and equipment; targets for energy production from non-fossil sources; and mandated caps on coal consumption.

China has added vast wind and solar installations to its grid and developed large domestic industries to manufacture solar panels, batteries and electric vehicles. In late 2017 it launched a national emissions trading system, which creates a market for buying and selling carbon dioxide emissions allowances. This was a profoundly symbolic step, given that the United States still has not adopted a national market-based climate policy.

Most of these policies will produce additional benefits, such as improving China's energy security, promoting economic reform and reducing ground-level air pollution. The only major program explicitly aimed at reducing carbon dioxide is the emissions trading system.

Major Challenges and Policy Gaps

Under the Paris Agreement, China committed to start reducing its carbon dioxide emissions and derive 20% of its energy from non-fossil fuels by around 2030. But when Chinese emissions rose in 2018, international observers feared that Beijing might fail to meet its targets. We analyzed China's actions to assess that risk.

In our review, we found that the policies with the greatest influence over China's projected emissions in 2030 were power sector reform, industrial transformation, industrial efficiency, emissions trading and light-duty vehicle efficiency.

Reforming the electric power sector is an essential step. Traditionally, electricity pricing schemes in China were determined by the National Development and Reform Commission, which leads the country's macroeconomic planning. They favored existing power producers, particularly coal plants, not the cleanest or most efficient sources.

China committed to electric power reform, including emission reductions and greater use of renewables, in 2015. Converting to a process under which grid managers buy electricity from generators starting with the lowest-cost sources should facilitate installation and use of renewables, since renewable electricity has almost zero marginal costs. Meanwhile, renewable energy projects across China, especially solar, have become cheaper than grid electricity.

Even as China made big investments in wind and solar power in recent years, it also kept building coal plants. Power sector reform will help reduce the resulting overcapacity by stopping planned additions and encouraging market competition.

But success is not guaranteed. The affected companies are giant state-owned enterprises. There is political resistance from owners of existing coal-fired power plants and from provinces that produce and use a lot of coal. The current U.S.-China trade war is slowing China's economic growth and spurring rising concerns about employment, which could further complicate the reform process.

China's emissions trading system has had a very modest impact so far because it set a low initial price on carbon dioxide emissions: US$7 per ton, increasing by 3% annually through 2030. But our analysis found that emissions trading, which allows low-carbon generators to make money by selling emissions allowances that they don't need, could become influential over the longer term if it can sustain a much higher price. If China reduces its cap on total carbon dioxide emissions after 2025, which will increase the price of emissions allowances, this policy could become a major driver for emission reductions in the power sector.

Energy efficiency standards, particularly for coal-fired power plants, factories and motor vehicles, will also be very important over the coming decade. To continue driving progress, China will need to update these standards continuously.

Finally, there are some important gaps in China's climate policies. Currently they only target carbon dioxide emissions, although China also generates significant quantities of other greenhouse gases, including methane and black carbon.

And China is contributing to emissions outside of its borders by exporting coal equipment and directly financing overseas coal plants through its Belt and Road Initiative. No nation, including China, currently reports emissions generated abroad in its national emissions inventory.

Following Through

The biggest challenge China faces in achieving its Paris targets is making sure that business and local governments comply with policies and regulations that the government has already put in place. In the past, China has sometimes struggled with environmental enforcement at the local level when provincial and city governments prioritized economic development over the environment.

Assuming that China does carry out its existing and announced climate and energy policies, we think its carbon dioxide emissions could likely peak well before 2030. In our view, Chinese leaders should focus on completing power sector reform as soon as possible, implementing and strengthening emissions trading, making energy efficiency standards more stringent in the future and developing new carbon pricing policies for sectors such as iron, steel and transportation.

If they succeed, U.S. politicians will no longer have "But what about China?" as an excuse for opposing climate policies at home.

America Is Losing Its Soft Power Advantage

Aynne Kokas and Oriana Skylar Mastro

Aynne Kokas is associate professor of media studies at the University of Virginia, a senior faculty fellow at the Miller Center for Public Affairs, and a nonresident scholar specializing in Chinese media at the Baker Institute of Public Policy at Rice University. Oriana Skylar Mastro is a Center Fellow at the Freeman Spogli Institute for International Studies at Stanford University and a fellow in foreign and defense policy studies at American Enterprise Institute (AEI).

The images of bare-chested, flag-waving MAGA loyalists overtaking the US Capitol flooded US social media and news channels in the days following the January 6 siege against the electoral college count. Memed and amplified, the same images circulated widely on Chinese social media and state-owned news sites without even the need for critical commentary.

The literal destruction of the US Capitol at the hands of President Donald Trump's followers required little imagination to characterize abroad as the downfall of American democracy.

There are many reasons for pessimism. According to one of the most authoritative indexes, Polity, the United States is no longer the world's oldest continuous democracy, dropping in status to a system that is part democracy, part dictatorship.

Beyond the domestic concerns faced in the aftermath of the breach of one of America's most hallowed buildings, the Capitol siege was a win for China. US soft power, one of its comparative advantages in the great power competition, has taken a huge hit.

Soft power is "the ability to get what you want through persuasion or attraction in the forms of culture, values, and policies." The US has been the primary beneficiary of soft

"The Soft War That America Is Losing," by Aynne Kokas and Oriana Skylar Mastro, *The Australian Financial Review*, January 15, 2021. Reprinted by permission.

power, with its globally recognized brands, pop culture, fast-food chains, world-renowned universities, and political values.

It is relatively low cost and high impact compared with other forms of power. The United States' relative attractiveness is one of the reasons America prevailed in the Cold War.

The Chinese government is having a propaganda field day. More than ever, the US *looks* like a country in decline, discouraging to allies and potential partners. Chinese commentators have noted that America's days as the "city on the hill" have come to an end. This is karma, some say, payback for the US supporting opposition groups, as in Hong Kong. As one netizen commented on the popular microblog website Weibo: "So lucky to be born in China."

China has also been trying to increase its soft power through traditional mechanisms such as building its media, education, and tourism sectors. It has enjoyed only moderate success in these areas because of its censorship, pollution, and lack of independent civil society.

But COVID-19 has led to the strengthening of other Chinese public diplomacy efforts, such as its landmark Belt and Road Initiative global trade and investment scheme.

Related initiatives such as the Digital Silk Road, a program to build out global digital infrastructure using Chinese technology, and the Health Silk Road, a plan to export Chinese health expertise through things such as COVID-19 laboratories and vaccine diplomacy, draw on China's comparative advantage in a top-down soft power approach.

Meanwhile, the Trump administration has undermined the historical sources of US soft power. It has shuttered visa lines, investigated international students on campus, and driven the rise of a culture of nationalism. The cancellation of the Fulbright US Student Program and the Peace Corps program in China are prime examples. And the COVID-19 decreased US media production, educational exchange and tourism, which shrank opportunities for promoting its democratic values on the global stage.

A bird's-eye view of America's relative soft power may seem to offer cause for optimism. Even after four years of Trump's buffoonery and "America First," the US is still far ahead of China, ranking fifth in overall soft power, while China ranks 24th. And isn't this what matters in competition?

Yes and no. The problem is two-fold. First, the US relies more on its political values as a soft power source than Beijing does. Ironically, this has especially been the case during the Trump administration. National Security Adviser Robert O'Brien has argued that democracies and authoritarian countries such as China "are offering a different approach to the world." Secretary of State Mike Pompeo has argued to international audiences that democracy is "what we've got right."

Second, Beijing has tried to leverage its comparative advantages to build soft power through pathways other than political values, especially where a top-down government approach is effective. China set up COVID-19 testing labs in Palestine in agreement with Israeli and Palestinian authorities. It extended its hand in Africa by building more than 70 percent of its 4G infrastructure.

Depending on need, useful solutions can be as compelling as political principles. The future of the US as a world leader is at stake. American military base access worldwide depends on perceived political alignment between the US and its allies. In the tech sector, the widespread adoption of US platforms relies on other countries finding that benefits to allowing in foreign platforms outweigh the potential political risks.

Successful multilateral treaty negotiations on issues such as global trade and climate change rely on the perception of a dependable US political system.

Strengthening democracy at home and moving away from "America First" policies will go a long way in reconstructing the trust and relationships central to soft power. But the United States will always be seen as a country in which the election of Donald Trump to the presidency, and now the storming of the Capitol, were possible.

President-elect Joe Biden will soon learn that soft power, once lost, may be difficult to revive.

Chinese Power and Its Discontents

Laura Silver, Kat Devlin, and Christine Huang

Laura Silver is an expert on international public opinion research and a senior researcher at Pew Research Center. Kat Devlin is a former researcher at Pew Research Center's Global Attitudes Project. Christine Huang is a research associate at Pew Research Center.

China has emerged as a global economic superpower in recent decades. It is not only the world's second largest economy and the largest exporter by value, but it has also been investing in overseas infrastructure and development at a rapid clip as part of its Belt and Road Initiative. A new Pew Research Center survey finds that, particularly in emerging markets, publics largely have a positive view of China's economic stature. People generally see China's growing economy as a good thing for their country and believe China is having a predominantly positive influence on their country's economic affairs.

But, even while China's rise is largely perceived as positive in emerging economies, there are pockets of discontent. First, even in the nations that welcome China's economic growth, few feel similarly about its growing military might. Rather, most tend to view China's growing military as something bad for their own countries. Second, China's neighbors generally take a much more negative stance toward China's military and economic growth than other countries surveyed. For example, in the Asia-Pacific region, more tend to see investment from China as a potential liability, giving Beijing too much influence over their economies. These same countries are also more likely than others to see U.S. economic influence in their country positively. And, when it comes to developed countries, views of China are much more mixed to

"China's Economic Growth Mostly Welcomed in Emerging Markets, but Neighbors Wary of Its Influence," by Laura Silver, Kat Devlin, and Christine Huang, Pew Research Center, December 5, 2019.

negative. Generally, countries with stronger human rights records and lower levels of corruption tend to be much less keen on China.

When it comes to comparisons with the United States, generally speaking, China's economic influence is seen in similar or even slightly more positive terms. Most publics are about equally sanguine about the state of their country's bilateral economic relations with China and the U.S. Majorities in most nations also say both the U.S. and China have a great deal or a fair amount of influence on their country's economic conditions. But, when rating that influence, more people say China's is positive than say the same of the U.S.

More still name the U.S. as the foremost economic power than say the same of China. For example, across every country surveyed in Latin America and sub-Saharan Africa, as well as many in the Asia-Pacific, people name the U.S. as the top economy. In the U.S., by a 50%-32% margin, Americans name their own country as the leading economic power, though there are stark partisan differences in these evaluations, with Republicans and Republican-leaning independents being more likely to name the U.S. than Democrats.

Most also prioritize relations with the United States—though this opinion is colored by perceptions of which economy is stronger. People who name the U.S. as the world's leading economy are more likely to prefer strong economic ties with the U.S., and the opposite is true when it comes to China. And, when it comes to alliances, many more name the U.S. as the top country their nation can rely on than China.

These are among the major findings from a Pew Research Center survey conducted among 38,426 people in 34 countries from May 13 to Oct. 2, 2019.

More Countries See U.S. As a Top Ally Than China

In many countries surveyed, the United States is viewed as an important ally. In Israel, 82% name the U.S. as the country they can most rely on as a dependable ally in the future. Across the Asia-Pacific region, around two-thirds or more cite the U.S. as a

top ally in Japan (63%), the Philippines (64%) and South Korea
(71%). In fact, in every country surveyed, more name the U.S. than
China—though opinion is relatively divided in several countries.

When it comes to which countries are most threatening,
though, both the U.S. and China emerge as top concerns across
the publics surveyed—though largely in different regions. Across
many of the Latin American as well as Middle East and North
African countries surveyed, more name the U.S. as a top threat
than say the same of China. The opposite is largely true in the
Asia-Pacific countries, where many more name China as a top
threat, including 40% of Australians, 50% of Japanese and 62% of
Filipinos. These countries are also among those that are most likely
to say China's growing military is a bad thing for their country—
though a median of 58% across the 18 countries polled generally
see downsides to a strengthening Chinese military.

Most Say Economic Relations with the U.S. and with China Are Positive

Across 17 countries, a median of 66% say their country's current
economic relations with China are good. Similarly high numbers (a
median of 64%) also rate current U.S. economic relations with their
countries favorably. In fact, in most countries polled, majorities
say current relations with each of the superpowers are good. For
example, 85% in Australia say U.S.-Australian economic relations
are in good shape, while 80% say the same of Sino-Australian ones.

In several countries people are likely to evaluate current
economic relations with one superpower positively, while seeing
the other in more negative terms. One such country, Canada, is
currently embroiled in trade tensions with China; people there
evaluate current economic relations with China 20 percentage
points less positively than those with the U.S. (even as trade
negotiations over the USMCA continue on). Countries on China's
periphery—including the Philippines, South Korea and Japan—
also view current economic relations with the U.S. much more
positively than relations with China. In some of the Middle East

and North African countries surveyed, the opposite is true. For example, only 42% of Lebanese say current economic relations with the U.S. are good, compared with 82% who say the same of China.

When it comes to whether the U.S. or China is having a positive or negative influence on each country's economic conditions, though, publics on balance are somewhat more approving of China's impact. A median of 48% say China is having a positive impact on economic conditions in their country, compared with 42% who say the same of the U.S.

In Latin America, sub-Saharan Africa and the Middle East and North Africa, more tend to rate China's influence positively than say the same of the U.S.—even in countries where both countries' roles are seen positively overall. One such example is Nigeria, where 69% say China's economic influence is positive and 49% say the same of the U.S. Most Asia-Pacific countries, however, tend to say American economic influence is more positive than China's.

International Views of China Vary Greatly, Colored by Economic Attitudes

Global views of China are, on balance, mixed. A median of 40% across 34 countries surveyed have a favorable view of China, while a median of 41% have an unfavorable view. But opinion varies considerably across the nations surveyed, from a high of 71% in Russia to a low of 14% in Japan.

Among a subset of 15 countries that were asked questions about global economic engagement in general and Chinese investment in particular, statistical modeling results indicate that views of China are related to these economic attitudes (for a more detailed explanation, see Appendix).

Views of China's economic strength play a role in overall evaluations of China. Generally speaking, saying that China is the world's leading economic power, that China's growing economy is good for one's own country, that current bilateral economic relations with the superpower are in good shape or that China's economic influence is good for one's country is associated with more positive views toward China, holding other factors constant. But having a higher percentage of imports coming from China is related to more negative views of China.

Greater economic satisfaction and openness to international investment are also related to more favorable views of China. Those who are more satisfied with their own domestic economy tend to have more positive opinions of China. Additionally, those who see it as a good thing when foreign companies buy domestic companies in their country or when foreign companies build domestic companies in their country tend to be more positively disposed toward China.

Few Express Confidence in President Xi

Views of Chinese President Xi Jinping are, on balance, negative across the 34 countries surveyed. A median of 45% say they lack confidence in him when it comes to world affairs, compared with a median of 29% who say they trust him to do the right thing. But opinions vary widely across regions. In the U.S., Canada and Western Europe, half or more in almost all countries say they have no confidence in Xi, whereas confidence is much higher in all three sub-Saharan African countries surveyed and tends to be higher in several of the Middle East and North African countries surveyed.

In the six Asia-Pacific countries surveyed, most have little confidence in Xi Jinping when it comes to world affairs. Just 29% have confidence in him to do what is right, which falls far short of the ratings for Japan's Shinzo or India's Narendra Modi. And in the Philippines, Indonesia, India and South Korea, nearly equal numbers have confidence in North Korean leader Kim Jong Un as in Xi.

Still, positive opinions of Xi have increased in many countries over recent years. Just since 2018, for example, confidence in him has increased markedly in Italy (up 10 percentage points), Mexico (up 13 points), Spain (+13) and Argentina (+14). Only in South Korea has confidence in him fallen by double digits since 2018, decreasing 12 points.

Regional Spotlight: Asia-Pacific Stands Out for More Negative Attitudes Toward China, Its Role

People in the Asia-Pacific region are generally negative in their views of China, and attitudes in many surveyed countries there have grown more negative in recent years. These countries are more critical of investment from China. Roughly half or more in each Asia-Pacific nation surveyed say Chinese investment is a bad thing because it gives China too much influence, ranging from 48% of Indonesians to 75% of Japanese. South Korea and Indonesia stand out as two countries in which fewer today see benefits from China's growing economy than said the same five years ago.

China's neighbors are especially wary of its military growth. A median of 79% across the region say China's growing military strength is bad for their country, including nine-in-ten in Japan and South Korea. This depth of concern with China's growth is mirrored in the relative primacy these countries place on their relations with the United States. In each country in the region, more name the U.S. as their most dependable ally than any other country in an open-ended question, including around two-thirds or more in Japan (63%), the Philippines (64%) and South Korea (71%). Each country in the region also prefers strong economic ties with the U.S. (a median of 64%) rather than China (26%)— and often by a wide margin. In Australia and South Korea, this is a reversal of 2015 opinion, when more preferred close economic relations with China.

China Mismanaged Its Relationship with the European Union

Xue Qing

Xue Qing is a journalist and researcher based in Beijing. She writes regularly for China Daily, *and her work has also been featured in the English edition of* Global Times.

In the past several months, the China-EU relationship has deteriorated to its lowest point since 1989. After the two sides exchanged sanctions over the Xinjiang issue, political disputes are jeopardizing the fate of the Comprehensive Agreement on Investment, which was celebrated by Chinese and European leaders just a few months ago and is seen as an important milestone in their relationship.

On May 20, the European Parliament decided to freeze the ratification of the agreement, announced that it will not proceed with the agreement until China lifts the sanctions it imposed on European NGOs and individuals, including several members of the European Parliament. The decision did not occur in a vacuum. The views of European political leaders and the public alike on China have become increasingly negative. Top European leaders admitted recently that there are "fundamental divergences" between the two giants, while a Pew survey shows that unfavorable views on China have reached record highs in many European countries. Although China and the EU are still fostering cooperation in areas such as climate change, this can barely save their relationship from a downward spiral.

The drastic fall of China-EU relations did not happen overnight. Both sides have been constantly calibrating their perception toward one another and redefining the other party's respective role in their overall external relations. This is

"How China Is Losing Europe," by Xue Qing, Diplomat Media Inc., May 25, 2021. Reprinted by permission.

particularly true for the EU. Recognizing China's fast-growing power, the EU began to call for a more equal and reciprocal relationship in terms of trade and investment with China in the early 2000s, and expected China to show more respect for democracy and human rights. However, these expectations were proven largely wishful thinking. China insisted on its unique economic system, maintained market-protection policies, and, in the eyes of Europeans, is becoming even more authoritarian. This triggered growing complaints and pessimism across Europe. However, such sentiments were little noticed in China until 2019, when the EU defined China as an "economic competitor" and "systemic rival."

Certainly, the relationship between China and Europe is shaped by the interaction between the two parties and is affected by external factors—the United States, in particular. However, their relationship was not inevitably doomed to become what it is now. From the perspective of China, there are at least three serious pitfalls in its policy on the EU.

First, China failed to treat the EU as a serious political and security actor. The EU is a superpower in many aspects. It is a strong economy and an important shaping force of the international order. It plays an important role in resolving global issues such as climate change and infectious diseases. Its member states, although they share a tight bond with the United States in the defense realm, are not security dwarfs. They are, together with the EU, key players in tackling security challenges in places such as Libya, the Sahel, Syria, and Ukraine. Besides, the EU holds strong soft power: It creates and leads multilateral institutions, formulates international regulations, and projects invisible influence around the globe. Today, the EU has put forward the concept of strategic autonomy and is trying to play a more decisive role in geopolitical games, demonstrating its growing ambition.

This should have been ample notice to Chinese policymakers. But they have been looking down on the EU and failed to recognize European power and ambition. Policymakers and observers in Beijing refuse to acknowledge the great success of European integration and its remarkable capability to deal with challenges at home and abroad. They take Brussels as a sheer talk shop and the EU as a fragile bloc with deep divides inside that could break into pieces any time.

In terms of foreign policy, China regards the United States as its primary, if not only, target for policymaking. Too often, Beijing looks at its relations with Europe in the context of China-U.S. and EU-U.S. relations, and hopes not to push the EU toward the Americans, so as to prevent the formation of an alliance against it. Chinese policymakers either underestimate the EU's will and capability or overestimate the EU's need for the United States. This old-fashioned view of European power and mindset of defining China-EU relations with regards to a third country distort China's European policy and cloud its understanding of the true EU.

Second, China failed to take the EU's normative appeals seriously. The EU, for decades, has been underlining the importance of values such as democracy, human rights, and rule of law in its external relations. Its relations with China are not an exception. However, China seems unable to understand and often does not care about the EU's normative concerns. From the perspective of practical interests, China puts more emphasis on investment and trade relations between the two parties, and when the normative divergences become prominent, it attempts to use the investment and trade "carrot" to "buy" the EU. China has long viewed the EU like a chihuahua that bites without inflicting serious harm, and will keep quiet for at least a while if given a bone. Such a trick indeed worked before, but it will not work always. Business is not the whole of bilateral relations. When norms and values become high on the political agenda, China should not naively believe that the EU will make a Faustian deal.

But China does not have to fight a normative war with the EU either, at least not now. As a result of being strong, China is now being scrutinized and that leads to the problem of "being scolded." Chinese leaders are annoyed with critics abroad and decided to build a more favorable and popular image on the world stage. But they should be aware that it takes skill and time, perhaps decades, to make such changes. Even then, improvements may diminish but will not eliminate critics. Chinese leaders should not dream of a world where other countries butter them up, like ancient Chinese emperors once enjoyed. It would be wise for them to start to learn to live with international critics, including those from Europe. Meanwhile, Chinese policymakers should do what they can, even the smallest things, to win foreign hearts and minds.

Third, China failed to develop more sophisticated diplomacy with the EU. China has changed rapidly and dramatically in the past decades. However, it seems that Beijing does not have a clear idea of its influence and potential threat to others, and thus acts slowly in responding to changes. In the case of its relations with the EU, China keeps declaring that it aims to establish a deep cooperative partnership with the EU, regardless of the changing perception the EU has of China. China behaves like an ostrich burying its head in the sand, refusing to fix its unpractical view and policy on the EU and recognize the important divergences between the two. But unfortunately, these divergences will not vanish because of China's ignorance. Instead, they will accumulate and eventually lead to greater troubles.

In addition, while Beijing finds that it has more power to defend its growing interests, foreign concerns over the way it applies that power continue to grow. In recent years, Chinese leaders have repeatedly called on their people to be more confident in their country and on diplomats to show more "fighting spirit." However, such confidence is becoming arrogance in some cases, while the "fighting spirit" is turning to sheer combative and hostile talk. In such context, Chinese diplomats are becoming "wolf warriors," and listening, understanding, or compromise might be seen as diffidence and cowardice. The China-EU relationship is one of the victims of that style of diplomacy. Chinese diplomats are flaming European foreign ministries, which only further ruins China's image among European policymakers and citizens.

To be fair, China is not solely to blame for the deterioration of China-EU relations. However, the carelessness and clumsiness of China's Europe policy undoubtedly contributed to the fall.

Chinese leaders have set ambitious development goals for 2035, striving to turn China into a modern country by that time. For China, there is nothing more important than reaching these goals. China learned a lot from the EU in the past 40 years of reform and opening up, and it can still do so in the next decades. China should treat the EU as a serious actor, a partner that can generate vital influence on China's fundamental interests. At the same time, Beijing must show more patience and leave other matters to time.

Questions About Chinese Data Transparency Linger

Ben S. Bernanke and Peter Olson

Ben S. Bernanke is a distinguished American economist. He served as chair of the Federal Reserve from 2006–14 and is currently a fellow at the Brookings Institution. Peter Olson is a research analyst at the Brookings Institution.

At the recent G20 gathering in Shanghai, three Chinese leaders— Premier Li Keqiang, People's Bank of China Governor Zhou Xiaochuan, and Finance Minister Lou Jiwei—reassured attendees that the Chinese government had the monetary and fiscal tools as well as the know-how to guide the economy through its current challenges. The success of the communications offensive, which seems to have calmed investor concerns for the moment, stands in strong contrast to the communications missteps that exacerbated adverse market reactions to the Chinese government's stock market and currency interventions over the past year.

These statements at the G20 suggest that Chinese officials are better understanding the need to clearly explain major policy initiatives—a difficult transition for a government accustomed to secrecy. However, communication of this sort represents only one form of transparency. In this post we discuss two other important forms that complement clear explanations by policymakers: data transparency (producing believable numbers), and transparency about the rules of the game (being clear about rules and policies that affect participants in commerce, the markets, etc.). For China to fulfill its potential as a global financial and economic leader, it needs to make further progress on these dimensions as well.

"China's Transparency Challenges," by Ben S. Bernanke and Peter Olson, The Brookings Institution, March 8, 2016. Reprinted by permission.

Data Transparency

On August 11, 2015, China simultaneously announced changes to
its exchange-rate regime and devalued its currency by 1.9 percent
against the dollar, a surprise move that sparked market selloffs.
Traders apparently inferred that the Chinese leadership knew
more than they did about Chinese growth prospects and had
devalued to offset weakening domestic demand with increased
exports. On the surface, there was no need to guess about Chinese
growth: Only a few weeks before, China had announced its second
quarter figure was right on target at 7.0%. But to many, this
announcement had seemed too good to be true, provoking a
flurry of skepticism in the international press.

Are China's growth numbers wrong? There is a lively debate
in the academic literature about the quality of key Chinese data.
A case can be made that China's National Bureau of Statistics
(NBS) deserves more credit than it is commonly given. For
example, while there is evidence that some official statistics are
"too smooth," this smoothness is unusual in that it includes a
long period of overstated inflation and understated growth, which
smacks of technical error more than political tampering. One
study found that the official growth numbers were "significantly
and positively correlated" with externally verifiable measures
of economic activity, including import and export data from
China's trading partners, and another found they were historically
only "weakly related," but that the official numbers have been
growing more accurate over time. Many researchers (including
those at international agencies like the World Bank) find the
official GDP data to be at least "usable and informative" [Feng,
Hu, and Moffitt].

The NBS has shown signs that it takes seriously its task of
providing reliable GDP numbers. As Carsten Holz of the Hong
Kong University of Science and Technology observes, the Bureau
has increasingly made a point of bypassing suspect provincial
reports by conducting its own surveys and relying on direct
relationships with firms and other reporting units. So why is there

so much skepticism? Because the main barrier to greater data credibility is structural—specifically, the lack of independence and transparency of the NBS and other Chinese data providers.

In the United States and other advanced economies, government statistical agencies are staffed by career professionals whose independence from politics is widely accepted. (The heads of some agencies are political appointees, but the individuals chosen are almost always themselves professional statisticians rather than politicians.) Moreover, the purveyors of official data provide extensive detail about the sources of data and the assumptions and analyses used. Indeed, the process of constructing U.S. GDP statistics, for example, is sufficiently transparent that even private forecasters can "nowcast" current-quarter data by replicating the process used by the U.S. Bureau of Economic Analysis. The combination of agencies' independence from politics and their transparency about methodologies and sources, more so than their resources or technical expertise, makes the official data in advanced economies highly credible.

Chinese data agencies don't have these advantages. For example, the NBS is a government department under the direct control of the Party and the State Council. The past several directors of the NBS have had doctorates in finance or economics, but their impartiality as statisticians is questioned because of what Holz calls a "near-perfect congruence between the Party leadership and the bureaucratic leadership within the NBS." (The NBS director is also its top party official.) The principle that data collection agencies should be independent has not gained much traction in China. Moreover, the NBS has little external authority and thus limited ability to set statistical standards for or requisition data from other agencies; consequently, it cannot assure the integrity of the data on which it relies.

China's statistical agencies also fall short on transparency. Notably, the NBS provides relatively little information about its source data or its statistical framework, making outside verification of its numbers, or an understanding of their strengths and weaknesses, essentially impossible. In particular, the NBS does not publish enough source data to allow researchers to replicate its GDP calculations.

The good news here is that China has a straightforward path to considerably increased data credibility, should it choose to take it: First, the NBS and other statistical agencies could be made substantially more independent, in both reality and perception, by appointing competent, unbiased technocrats; by developing a culture of independence at the agencies, supported by a clear mandate to provide the most accurate data possible; and by making the NBS the official setter of standards for economic data, with the ability to audit data sources and to request information from other agencies. Second, greater transparency about source data and methods, including the possibility of outside peer review, would help reassure users of the quality and objectivity of the data, while clarifying the areas where further improvement is needed. In short, to increase the credibility of Chinese economic data, increase the credibility of the data collectors.

"Rules of the Game" Clarity

China's main stock index more than doubled from November 2014 to June 2015, which led a nervous China Securities Regulatory Commission (CSRC) to limit one type of margin borrowing. This precipitated a 2% one-day fall in the index, which led to further declines as traders were forced to sell stocks they'd bought on margin. The CSRC then responded with "a succession of desperate measures: it suspended initial public offerings, allowed companies to stop trading, and limited short selling," notes leading Chinese economist Yu Yongding. "It even organized a 'national team' of 21 large securities companies, led by a government-controlled financial corporation, to purchase shares." Yongding notes: "In doing so, China's regulatory authority changed many well-established rules of the game virtually overnight."

Market participants saw many of the actions taken as clumsy; even worse, the interventions and others that followed seemed arbitrary and unpredictable. Certainly, many Westerners concluded that they would not participate in the Chinese market, at least not until the rules of the game were clearly laid out. In general, the absence of clear and transparent rules and policies—in financial markets, as well as for activities such as commerce, capital investment, and trade—is a major problem because it dissuades participation, adds uncertainty, and can even foster corruption.

On the real-economy side, China has committed to some transparent rule-making. The U.S.-China Business Council (USCBC), in its 2015 Regulatory Transparency Scorecard, noted that "all of China's economic and trade-related central government agencies have agreed to public comment periods of at least 30 days on draft laws, administrative regulations, departmental rules, and regulations that function as regulations and rules." These commitments were made in stages—some back when China joined the World Trade Organization (WTO) in 2001, some in bilateral dialogues with the U.S. These commitments apply, for example, to rulings by the National People's Congress (NPC) and the State Council, in addition to other important bodies. The USCBC's assessment is that China has made some progress in fulfilling these commitments but has some distance to go. For example, according to the Council, in 2014 the People's Congress made available for public comment three of the nine laws it passed. The State Council posted 75 percent of the required regulatory documents on its website, using a narrow definition of what is covered by the agreement, or 30 percent with a broader definition of what is covered. However, many of the documents posted were made available too late for comment by affected parties.

Another example of commitments China has made—which it is partially fulfilling—comes from a report released by the office of the U.S. Trade Representative (USTR) a few months ago. When China joined the WTO, it agreed to publish all trade-related laws and regulations in a single official journal. According to the USTR, "some but not all central-government entities publish trade-related measures in this journal," and "these government entities tend to take a narrow view" of what must be included. Similarly, the USTR claimed that China's rulemaking process remained inconsistent and that those affected did not always have a chance to comment on proposed rules.

Clarity about the rules of the game doesn't necessarily mean that the rules are either simple or fair. Indeed, US regulations are riddled with complexities. However, U.S. rules are publicly available and are developed through open processes. Though not sufficient, this seems necessary for well-functioning markets and institutions. It would be in China's interest to prioritize rules-of-the-game transparency.

Conclusion

There is great value in good communication about policy. Indeed, in the words of a recent *Wall Street Journal* article, investors are putting "more clarity from China's central bank over its currency policy and better communication from its stock-market regulator" at the "top of their wish list."

But transparency is more than press conferences. Data transparency provides investors, the public, and even Chinese policymakers greater confidence about the state of the economy, and transparency about the rules of the game is critical for the economy and for financial markets. The more transparency and consistency the Chinese government can provide in these spheres, the better will be China's economic performance and the greater its ability to integrate with the global marketplace.

CHAPTER 2

Will the Withdrawal from Afghanistan Diminish American Credibility and Influence Around the World?

Overview: US Policy in the Years Ahead Will Determine the Legacy of the War in Afghanistan

Nilofar Sakhi and Annie Pforzheimer

Nilofar Sakhi is a nonresident senior fellow at the Atlantic Council's South Asian Center and a lecturer at George Washington University's Elliott School of International Affairs. Annie Pforzheimer is a nonresident associate with the Center for Strategic and International Studies and an adjunct professor at the City University of New York (CUNY).

As the United States exits from Afghanistan, on the eve of the 20th anniversary of the 9/11 attacks, it is important to reflect on the broader and longer-term reverberations of that withdrawal. In examining the withdrawal, peace process, and the recent dynamic of militia building and Taliban control, it's becoming clear that a different transnational threat to U.S. interests is emerging.

The U.S. has been mistaken in believing the Afghanistan war was ours to direct, and we are mistaken now if we think it is ours to "end." The conflict has just entered a new phase with the international troop withdrawal. Instead of an environment we can help manage, the U.S. will be buffeted by the consequences of the predatory behavior of Afghanistan's neighbors and non-state terror organizations. We now have nuclear-armed states competing for influence in Afghanistan with no NATO presence to mitigate their ferocity. We failed this test in the 1990s and paid for it in 2001. With that in mind, the best course for the U.S. is to reengage, rather than renege on our commitments, in order to protect our interests in this important region.

"Missing the Bigger Implications of US Withdrawal from Afghanistan," by Nilofar Sakhi and Annie Pforzheimer, Middle East Institute, July 29, 2021. Reprinted by permission.

Security Threats

The overall objectives of the 2001 U.S. intervention in Afghanistan were to fight the parties responsible for the 9/11 attacks—al-Qaeda and the Taliban government—and ensure that Afghanistan could not be used as a safe haven for groups that threatened U.S. security. But these threats have been resilient. In a recent interview, al-Qaeda operatives promised, "War against the U.S. will be continuing on all other fronts unless they are expelled from the rest of the Islamic world."

A new level of uncertainly and instability has emerged with the news and deadline of the U.S. withdrawal, and no concrete plan or measure is in place for counterterrorism. With one-third of the country under Taliban control, high levels of violence are concerning. Unknown peace prospects send the message that the Taliban may seek to embark on a military takeover, which could result in a civil war. Terror groups like the Islamic State-Khorasan Province (ISKP) in the eastern provinces of Afghanistan and targeted killings by the Taliban generate fear among the educated and professionals for their survival. This has resulted in a new wave of Afghan migration, particularly of the highly skilled population. The deteriorating security situation will further divide the political factions in Afghanistan and invite regional players to join the conflict, fueling the proxy war and creating space for violent extremism to emerge and thrive.

Over the last 20 years, terrorist groups have patiently exploited opportunities to exert themselves. Global politics and enabling conditions for regional alliance building have given them the traction they needed in Iraq, Syria, the Sahel, and elsewhere. In addition, ungoverned or ill-governed physical areas and inadequate governance capacity allowed them to plan, communicate, and operate at opportune times. Radical movements have expanded their influence in various localities, resulting in ideologies that contradict the systems that promote an open society and its values. The Taliban have been ambiguous about their plans for a political settlement, stating only that they envision an Islamic system that embraces all Afghans. But they are clearly fighting for the restoration of an emirate similar to one they ruled in the 1990s, alarming those who experienced their authoritarian system. Reports highlight that the Taliban still have links to al-Qaeda and ISIS, which further exacerbates the security situation and shows how a Taliban victory would help strengthen transnational terrorist groups.

Regional Consequences

The insecurity in Afghanistan raises major concerns among its neighbors, particularly as threats of cross-border militancy and drug trafficking reach their borders and affect internal security and stability. The regional actors in Central Asia are especially on edge, as the recent surge in violence in Afghanistan affects certain border areas in the country's northern provinces. This includes the escalation in armed conflict on the Tajik-Afghan border, which made Moscow step in and offer its support to Tajikistan. For the sake of their own security, these countries don't want a direct armed conflict or high-level insurgency in Afghanistan. The relationship between Central Asian countries and Afghanistan continues to be cordial, with the former expressing their ambitions for cooperation through bilateral agreements to expand trade, development, and diplomatic relationships. But without some level of security and stability in Afghanistan, such bilateral agreements will remain mere written documents that cannot be realized.

The next and the most important player in Afghan war and peace is Pakistan, which believes the Taliban are set for victory. After 20 years of support, the Pakistanis see this as their own win.

There is also a general belief among some observers that the U.S. will eventually outsource Afghanistan to Pakistan, opening the door to political engagement and economic incentives between the U.S. and Pakistan. However, such a deal will concern India, which worries about the potential security threats that a Pakistan-supported Taliban could pose. Islamabad and New

Delhi strive to impede each other's political influence in Kabul, and their policy of engagement will take into consideration this common objective.

At this point the uncertainty in Afghanistan makes it hard for New Delhi to cement its policy of engagement. If India sees Pakistan control and influence Afghanistan, there will be a new phase of conflict between them inside Afghanistan, which will further aggravate the instability and insecurity and only add more elements of radicalization and violent extremism.

In addition, as Taliban victories on the battlefield grow, all other factions will ramp up their efforts to build militias and create an opposing force to defeat them. Expect regional powers to arm and supply money to their preferred factions and for the militias to keep switching sides and loyalties for gains that will further weaken the Afghan central government. If the Afghan government holds after the U.S. withdrawal, countries like China and India will be more active in Afghan affairs. If the Taliban capture power and the government, Pakistan's influence will increase significantly.

Iran, Russia, and China remain ambivalent about the U.S. withdrawal and will hold off to see how Afghanistan's political landscape changes. The United States has been in constant negotiations with regional players for security and counterterrorism assurances, but the regional players have a price tag for those demands. This includes security assurances and resources that will allow their economic gains.

In the current context, Russia intends to play a leading role in developing a regional consensus on Afghanistan's future power structure through an expanded "troika" alongside the United States, China, and Pakistan; China already announced that the Belt and Road Initiative will extend to Afghanistan, after saying in 2019 that it will enhance connectivity by extending the China-Pakistan Economic Corridor (CPEC). China's success in these endeavors depends upon stability. So it will strive to play a convening role to ensure some level of security for realization of its economic interests in Central and Southwest Asia. Meanwhile, the Afghan government may reach out to China to supersede the U.S. presence at Bagram and fill the vacuum left by the Americans' withdrawal.

Where Does This Leave Us?

With the deteriorating security situation, the security-centric interests of these countries may lead them to forge stronger diplomatic and security ties with each other. The regional powers are likely to ask for assurances from the Taliban to refrain from harboring extremists and favor their economic interests. To that end, they may take a lead in Afghan peace making. Tehran's recent hosting of Taliban-Afghan government talks and earlier negotiations hosted by Moscow demonstrate that the regional powers are aware that the Taliban will hold power in a matter of months or years, therefore building a relationship with them at this critical time opens the door for future bargaining. All these factors add up to one dispiriting reality: the U.S. government— and the American people—cannot simply wipe the dust off our hands, ship out of Afghanistan, and never look back. To be fair, President Joe Biden has indicated we will remain engaged with Afghanistan through security and development assistance, and through our diplomacy. But the details of those efforts largely remain to be seen, and America's eagerness to put the 20-year experience in Afghanistan behind us suggests there will be little, if any, urgency to conduct more than an arms-length involvement there.

We can and must do better. Of immediate priority, we should:

- Continue our critical support for the Afghan security forces, which are now the only remaining check on the Taliban that is not a criminal or self-defense mob. While doing that we have to also engage NATO to continue its support and partnership, especially for the police. This support has to be targeted, focusing on the contractors who keep the

Afghan military wing flying and defensive intelligence to keep the Taliban out of the cities and fight ISKP.

- Maintain existing U.N. and U.S. sanctions on Taliban leaders because lifting them would truly send the message that all international human rights rules are simply fiction. Expand those sanctions too, including new U.N. listings for those who are "destabilizing Afghanistan," as U.N. Security Council Resolution 1988 qualifies for listings, or U.S. listings such as the "kingpin" designation for those who are profiting from the drug trade, which the latest U.N. report indicates is the "Taliban's largest single source of income."

- Seek and coalesce the involvement of Afghanistan's neighbors—especially those hedging right now and supporting all sides to the conflict—to instead support good outcomes in Afghanistan, and work through the U.N. Security Council to empower effective mediation mechanisms. Invite strategic adversaries, such as Russia, Iran, and China, to help set the terms of this international role—or be forced to simply cede this region (including Central Asia) to their control.

- Enhance regional connectivity and Afghanistan's fragile economy via a multilateral development package, including transportation infrastructure, to incentivize Afghanistan's neighbors to trade via land routes.

- Continue engagement and presence in regional meetings to combat transnational terrorist groups that currently or potentially operate in Afghanistan.

- Condition U.S. development aid to Taliban-controlled areas on the Taliban ending their violence, committing to a comprehensive nationwide cease-fire, entering into good faith negotiations, and adhering to international human rights standards; and avoid allowing humanitarian aid to be labeled as coming from the Taliban.

- Publicly condemn Taliban and warlord aggression against constitutional rights for girls, women, and other vulnerable communities in Afghanistan.
- Protect the many Afghans who are vulnerable to killings or repression by the Taliban because they gave support to the U.S. and NATO allies, including providing them with special visas to come to the U.S. or to other safe destinations, and protecting human rights defenders and prominent women and minority leaders.
- Most importantly, communicate with the American and Afghan publics about detailed U.S. plans to stand by its ally, to achieve these goals, and to follow through on them as assiduously and urgently as possible. Potential allies worldwide are watching us.

The complex and competing motives driving many others who will fill the void left in the wake of disengagement in Afghanistan suggest an ominous future for the people of Afghanistan, the region, and, indeed, American strategic interests. We may think we are shutting the door on our difficult 20 years in Afghanistan, but before long we will have little choice but to respond to what's happening behind it.

How China Could Benefit from the US Withdrawal from Afghanistan

Lt. Gen. Richard P. Mills and Erielle Davidson

Lt. Gen. Richard P. Mills served as commander of the Marine Forces Reserve and Marine Forces North. Erielle Davidson is a senior policy analyst at the Jewish Institute for the National Security of America (JINSA) and a staff writer at The Federalist.

Each time the world's most powerful country admits some degree of failure, it is inevitable that such a decision will have sweeping—and lasting—consequences. The United States' withdrawal from Afghanistan, ending a two-decades-long presence, will be no exception. The decision undoubtedly sets a dangerous precedent for the future.

The Afghanistan withdrawal—and abandonment of the Afghanistan government and civilians to the Taliban's onslaught—has been publicly justified as a means for the United States to focus on other arenas of concern, namely great power competition with China in the Indo-Pacific region. While China might indeed be the graver threat, it is myopic to believe that the United States' ability to address that challenge will be unaffected by its disastrous exit from Afghanistan.

The most immediate and devastating consequence of the United States' exit is the fall of Kabul and the takeover of the country by the Taliban, as Afghan government troops fled the Taliban's arrival or surrendered. In their sweep through the country, the Taliban have carried out organized executions, closed schools, and forced unmarried girls and women to be paired off with Taliban fighters.

Though this might seem like a tragic plight for Afghans, but one far away from American shores, the U.S. abandonment of

"How the Afghan Withdrawal Impacts US-China Competition," by Lt. Gen. Richard P. Mills (ret.) and Erielle Davidson, *Defense News*, September 17, 2021. Reprinted by permission.

Afghanistan will have both direct and indirect consequences for U.S. national security.

The result of the Taliban instituting an Islamic emirate in the totality of Afghanistan will be a murderous regime that may well end up being an epicenter of terrorism in the region. Twenty years ago, the Taliban allowed Afghanistan to serve as the planning and training hub for global terror attacks. With their return, another wave of terror, and maybe another significant attack on America, once again becomes possible. As the U.S. Treasury Department wrote earlier this year: "Al-Qaeda is gaining strength in Afghanistan while continuing to operate ... under the Taliban's protection."

Through diplomatic channels, the United States must emphasize that we will not tolerate a sanctuary for terrorists to exist anywhere in the world, including in the Taliban's nascent regime in Afghanistan.

But the long-term geopolitical consequences of U.S. withdrawal vis-à-vis China are becoming increasingly apparent, as well. If the objective is to refocus U.S. resources on besting China, our withdrawal does the precise opposite by providing fertile ground for China's expansionist ambitions. The U.S. departure from Afghanistan creates a large opening for Beijing to execute on its geostrategic aims, which range from capitalizing on Afghanistan's supply of rare earth metals, estimated to be worth $1 trillion to $3 trillion, to undermining perceptions of a U.S.-led world order.

It is no surprise that China has been busy constructing thoroughfares between China and Afghanistan in order to absorb Afghanistan into Beijing's larger Belt and Road Initiative.

Though China remains wary of Taliban control, the lukewarm relationship between the Taliban and Beijing signals China's initial efforts to bring Afghanistan into its orbit—and to use the growing chaos and violence (which the U.S. withdrawal quickened) as a justification for doing so. To counter these efforts, the United States should be conducting a strong messaging campaign against China, communicating to the Muslim world that China's treatment of the Uyghurs shows most emphatically that Beijing is not a friend to those of the Islamic faith, as most of the ethnic group identifies as Muslim.

Finally, the U.S. withdrawal sends a sobering message to allies and partners of the United States in Central Asia and the Middle East: America has become increasingly unreliable. Countries that count on the United States as part of their larger national security strategy, which often includes the deterrence umbrella of the United States, may infer from America's Afghanistan "bugout" that the United States doesn't have the stamina to fulfill its long-term security commitments.

It makes little sense to perturb lasting allies at a time when U.S. strategy demands the maintenance (and development of) alliances to contain China, especially in the instance of Taiwan and Israel (U.S. partners that routinely face different forms of political and economic pressure from China). Furthermore, others may think twice before adopting and assisting us in our geostrategic objectives. In the worst-case scenario, our unreliability may send countries straight into the orbit of China.

We must reassure our allies, especially those in NATO, that they will continue to have our support and that their security remains a top priority, and we must reinforce such statements by maintaining our forward-deployed presence globally.

The immediate consequences of instability and violence, combined with the long-term consequence of casting doubt on America's credibility, suggest the U.S. withdrawal will serve only to thwart its goal of checking Chinese expansionism by quickening Afghanistan's descent into chaos and alienating historically committed U.S. partners and allies.

"America is back" has frequently been touted when emphasizing that potentially fractured relationships with U.S. partners will be restored. But the overwhelming message of our Afghanistan withdrawal likely will be that America does not have its partners' backs.

The Afghan Withdrawal Will Damage American Credibility

Matthew Kroenig and Jeffrey Cimmino

Matthew Kroenig is a professor of government at the Edmund T. Walsh School of Foreign Service at Georgetown University. Jeffrey Cimmino is assistant director at the Atlantic Council and assistant director of the Global Strategy Initiative at the Scowcroft Center for Strategy and Security.

Following the swift and dramatic fall of Kabul to the Taliban, the U.S. government and outside analysts are rightly focused on the immediate crisis, including safely evacuating U.S. personnel. When the dust settles, however, it will become clear that America's loss in Afghanistan will have much more important and far-reaching strategic consequences to which Washington must also attend. Indeed, America's retreat from Afghanistan risks undermining several of President Biden's own most important foreign policy priorities.

Biden has emphasized his desire for the United States to resume its global leadership role, repeatedly saying that "America is back." U.S. global leadership and the stability of the international system depend, in large part, on Washington's promises to protect friends and defend against enemies. More than 30 formal treaty allies, which combine to make up more than half of global GDP, rely on American security guarantees. If the United States cannot be trusted to keep its word, however, then allies may find it prudent to find other ways to protect themselves and adversaries may see a green light to aggress without consequence.

Unfortunately, the U.S. retreat in Afghanistan will deal a significant blow to U.S. credibility. The United States spent 20 years promising to build a self-sufficient democratic government in that

"The Strategic Consequences of America's Loss in Afghanistan," by Matthew Kroenig and Jeffrey Cimmino, *The Dispatch*, August 17, 2021. Reprinted by permission.

country. It failed. With Washington reneging on the promises it made to the Afghan people for two decades, will others trust its word? NATO allies, which worked alongside the United States to defeat the Taliban and rebuild the country, also felt blindsided by Biden's decision. Already questions are being raised about American reliability. Rivals in Moscow and Beijing are gloating, and even Washington's closest friends are concerned. "Whatever happened to 'America is back'?" asked Tobias Ellwood, chair of the Defense Committee in the British Parliament. "The Western democracy that seemed to be the inspiration for the world, the beacon for the world, is turning its back," said Rory Stewart, Britain's former minister for international development.

Beyond lost credibility, there is the status of global democracy and human rights. The emerging Biden doctrine sees a world at an "inflection point" in a struggle between democracies and autocracies. According to Biden, "We must demonstrate that democracies can still deliver for our people. That is our galvanizing mission."

But in its hasty retreat from Afghanistan, the United States has abandoned a fledgling democratic government and handed power to a Taliban theocracy. The failed democratic experiment in Kabul will rightly lead the Afghan people and others to question whether democracy really can deliver. Afghanistan's backslide into autocracy will be another data point in worrying trend lines showing a global decline in the number of democracies globally over each of the past 15 years. Taliban rule is already leading to gross human rights abuses on the ground, including executions and rape, and these practices and others, tragically, will likely become the new normal there.

Finally, the Biden administration has vowed to focus on great power competition with China, with Secretary of State Antony Blinken calling China's rise America's "biggest geopolitical test of the 21st century." Some proponents of the withdrawal from Afghanistan argued that this would free up forces and resources that could be directed toward competition with Beijing. But U.S.

withdrawal, on balance, will weaken America's position vis-à-vis China.

The aforementioned battered U.S. credibility will affect Beijing's calculations about whether Washington has the stomach to defend U.S. allies in the Indo-Pacific, possibly making a Chinese invasion of Taiwan more tempting. Moreover, the United States squandered significant influence in Central and South Asia, with U.S. adversaries Russia, China, and Iran filling the vacuum and forging warm relations with the new Taliban government. Finally, the U.S. military position in the continent will be diminished as it abandons Bagram Air Base and other key military installations, reducing U.S. options for posturing forces against China and the future terrorist threats that are likely to re-emerge in a Taliban-ruled Afghanistan.

The rapid fall of Kabul and disorganized U.S. retreat is an embarrassment for U.S. foreign policy, but, more than that, it severely undermines President Biden's own foreign policy agenda. After it addresses the immediate crisis, the Biden administration should pivot to mitigating the negative strategic consequences that come from losing America's longest war. A failure to do so effectively will damage Biden's agenda and U.S. global standing.

The Withdrawal from Afghanistan Reflects a Sound Reappraisal of US National Security Priorities

Vanda Felbab-Brown

Vanda Felbab-Brown is a senior fellow of the Center for Security, Strategy, and Technology and director of the Initiative on Nonstate Armed Actors at the Brookings Institution. She is the author of The Extinction Market: Wildlife Trafficking and How to Counter It *(Hurst, 2018).*

The Biden administration's decision to withdraw all U.S. troops from Afghanistan by September 11, 2021, is a wise strategic choice that took significant political courage. The administration correctly assessed that perpetuating U.S. military engagement in Afghanistan has become a strategic liability and a futile investment that lost the capacity to alter the basic political and military dynamics in Afghanistan. That does not mean that desirable political and security developments will follow in Afghanistan after the U.S. military withdrawal. Unfortunately, the possibility of an intensified and potentially highly fragmented and bloody civil war is real, and at minimum, the Taliban's ascendance to formal power will bring painful changes to the country's political dispensation.

The basic wisdom of the administration's decision is the realization that perpetuating U.S. military engagement would not reverse these dynamics and that U.S. military, financial, diplomatic, and leadership resources would be better spent on other issues. Even so, the administration made some serious tactical mistakes in its announcement.

"The US Decision to Withdraw from Afghanistan Is the Right One," by Vanda Felbab-Brown, The Brookings Institution, April 15, 2021. Reprinted by permission.

Strategic Priorities and Liabilities

The U.S. primary objective in Afghanistan since 2001 has been to degrade the threat of terrorism against the United States and its allies. That basic goal was accomplished a decade ago: Al-Qaida's capabilities are a fraction of what they used to be. The Islamic State in Khorasan (ISK) continues to operate in Afghanistan, but the Taliban has been fighting ISK assiduously. However, perpetually bad governance in Afghanistan has undermined stability and allowed the Taliban to entrench itself. While the Taliban too is implicated in many illicit economies, it is often seen as less predatory and capricious, even if brutal and restrictive, than powerbrokers associated with the Afghan government.

The Biden administration correctly assessed that the threat of terrorism from Afghanistan today is in fact smaller than from various parts of Africa and the Middle East. In Somalia, for example, al-Shabab's territorial and governing power are steadily increasing and the group retains a strong allegiance to al-Qaida. The Islamic State (ISIS) in Somalia, while much weaker than al-Shabab, retains persistent capacity. Various al-Qaida and ISIS affiliates robustly operate in Mali and other parts of the Sahel and North Africa. Thus, even though the Taliban is unwilling to sever its connections with al-Qaida, that threat is not radically different from the terrorist threats against the United States and our allies emanating from other locales. Though hopefully the U.S.-Taliban Doha agreement from February 2020 will incentivize the Taliban to prevent al-Qaida from taking actions against the United States and its allies from Afghanistan, and ongoing U.S. policy should be geared toward this objectives through diplomacy, conditional aid and sanctions, and, even, possibly occasional strikes from off-shore.

Moreover, U.S. veterans of such frustrating unending wars are an important source of right-wing armed recruitment in the United States and the threat to public safety, democracy, and rule of law those groups pose here. By minimizing such U.S.

military engagements abroad, the United States is taking a step in addressing this important danger.

The Biden administration's political courage lies in its refusal to be cowed by the possibility that a terrorism threat will grow in Afghanistan after the U.S. withdrawal. That specter has been a key justification for militarily staying on and on. That possibility needs to be weighed against other already materialized strategic threats and realities. Indeed, another wise aspect of the Biden administration's decision was to stop treating U.S. Afghanistan policy in isolation from other issues and strategic priorities; to date, the tyranny of sunk costs has inflated Afghanistan's importance.

Now, threats from China, an aggressive Russia, North Korea, and Iran—as well as zoonotic pandemics—are more important strategic priorities. Investing in U.S. Special Operation Forces, top leadership attention, and financial resources to counter those threats can deliver far greater strategic benefits than perpetuating the Afghanistan military effort.

The Hard Ground Realities in Afghanistan

The United States hasn't achieved its goal of defeating the Taliban. For several years, the Taliban has been steadily ascendant on the battlefield. It is on a path to become the strongest political force in Afghanistan, and a powerful actor in a future Afghan government.

Continuing the U.S. deployment won't alter this reality. There is no credible path whereby a sustained U.S. troop presence helps bring a desirable peace deal—"desirable" defined as a Colombia-like deal, with minimal political representation for the Taliban in national and subnational government, an amnesty, and fighter demobilization and reintegration assistance. In Colombia, the war was stalled at a much lower level of conflict when negotiations with the leftist guerrillas began, and the basic trends for the Revolutionary Armed Forces of Colombia (FARC) were headed downward. The opposite is the case in Afghanistan, where Afghan security forces by and large remain weak, often reach accommodation with the Taliban, and suffer from many deficiencies.

The U.S. military presence has slowed the Taliban's military and political gains, but not reversed them (even when American troop levels were 100,000 strong). It has no prospect of accomplishing them with 5,000 or 10,000 troops staying for another five or 10 years, let alone less. Since 2015, the U.S. approach to Afghanistan has been staying and praying—praying that the Taliban will make enough strategic mistakes to do itself in on the battlefield. It has not.

Nor has the United States managed to redress another key malady of Afghanistan: the perpetually parochial, fractious, and corrupt political elite, which engages in disruptive politicking instead of governing, even as Afghanistan has burned in an intensifying insurgency. Neither U.S. and international donor threats to reduce aid nor the ever-clearer and nearer prospect of the U.S. military withdrawal have swayed politicians toward unity against the Taliban and fundamentally improved governance.

Moreover, sustaining a U.S. military deployment in Afghanistan until a peace deal is reached would neglect the fact that any serious negotiations amidst the ground realities require the Afghan government to cede a considerable amount of power to the Taliban. The Afghan government has naturally not wanted to do so, and thus had had no interest in seriously negotiating with the Taliban. As long as there was a prospect for the United States staying militarily and propping up the Afghan government, Kabul has had little incentive to negotiate. Conversely, a firm U.S. withdrawal date—which Trump and now Biden have declared—incentivizes the Taliban not to negotiate until after U.S. troops are gone and the Taliban gains more power.

Supporters of a sustained presence point out that the U.S. withdrawal is abrupt; rather, Washington has repeatedly and ever more strongly signaled it over a decade. In 2014, for instance, the Obama administration was on the verge of going merely to an embassy-level military presence. But the Afghan government and political elites have ignored the steady warnings, hoping instead to entangle the United States with an open-ended military commitment until the Taliban was much weakened, however many years or decades that would take.

NATO and Pakistan

Even though the writing has been on the wall, the U.S. decision creates discomfort for some European allies—a poignant and ironic disparity in policy preferences. For years, the United States had been urging NATO allies under the International Security Assistance Force (ISAF) to devote greater military forces to Afghanistan and to leave their bases to engage in offensive counterinsurgency actions, even though Washington originally sold the Afghanistan mission to them as one of defensive patrolling, state-building, and economic development. Watching allies' restrictive battlefield rules of engagement made U.S. soldiers joke bitterly that ISAF stood for "I Saw America Fight," while U.S. troops slugged out in hard firefights in remote forward operating bases.

Yet while NATO partners are dependent on the United States for intelligence, surveillance, and reconnaissance and logistics—and thus are most unlikely to maintain a military presence in Afghanistan beyond the U.S. withdrawal—they now fear the withdrawal. The likely deterioration of security and political dispensation in Afghanistan creates serious domestic political problems for them, as does the prospect of Afghan refugees. But extending the withdrawal deadline from May 1 to September gives the NATO partners a chance to manage an orderly lift out from Afghanistan.

With Pakistan, U.S. policy can move toward more normalization. At a minimum, the withdrawal of U.S. forces from Afghanistan will liberate the United States from dependence on ground and air lines of control to Afghanistan through Pakistan. This dependence has been holding other elements of

U.S. Pakistan policy hostage, including concerns about tactical nuclear weapons, civil-military relations, and democracy.

The Bleak Outlook in Afghanistan

The political prospects in Afghanistan are not pretty. At best, the existing civil war, killing tens of thousands of Afghans annually, will eventually ease. But the Taliban is heading to power and the new political dispensation will mean a significant weakening of political and human rights, civil liberties, and pluralistic processes.

The Taliban continues to object to elections, at least elections that could remove it from power. Instead, it embraces an Iran-like model of a supreme religious council where the Taliban is the strongest actor, ruling over other political and administrative structures where elections can take place.

Understandably, the Taliban also wants to integrate its fighters into the Afghan military and intelligence services—whether or not the Afghan security forces have significantly collapsed beforehand. Already, the Taliban encircles at least 12 provincial capitals, and without the U.S. air power holding back its offensives, the Taliban can pounce on and hold many of them. Worse yet, the existing civil war can easily intensify into a far bloodier, fragmented, and protracted one (à la Syria or Libya) before the Taliban arrives in power, for who knows how long.

All of these likely losses to democratic processes, rights, and humanitarian concerns are immensely tragic. But the United States could no longer reverse them.

A Major Tactical Error and Way Forward

Although correct in its basic strategic decision, the Biden administration nonetheless made a major tactical error: In announcing the new withdrawal timeline just a few days before a planned Istanbul conference on Afghanistan, it undercut peace diplomacy. The conference—which sought an interim peace agreement between the Ashraf Ghani government and the Taliban, against the two sides' preferences—had been a major diplomatic stretch. The United States and the international community put a lot of diplomatic capital into a rushed and undercooked effort, further weakening the embattled Afghan government and augmenting the fractious tendencies among the Afghan elite.

Managed differently, the conference could have generated a new negotiating process, complementing the moribund Doha peace negotiations between the Afghan government and the Taliban. Unsurprisingly, the Taliban said this week that it would not engage in any peace conference until after all international troops are out of Afghanistan. This U.S. tactical error is costly for future American and international diplomatic efforts in Afghanistan.

The United States needs to remain engaged in those efforts and continually urge power-sharing in Afghanistan. It should continue providing financial, intelligence, and perhaps other remote support for the Afghan security forces. It should seek to shape the Taliban through prospects of international economic aid (or its denial), sanctions, travel visas, and other tools so as to minimize the losses to pluralistic political and economic processes and rights in Afghanistan. Those losses are coming, but we should try to reduce their extent. The United States should also mitigate humanitarian consequences, including by providing visas to Afghans who collaborate in the U.S. effort.

Despite the inglorious departure, having the wisdom to liquidate unwise commitments and redirect resources toward more important priorities is a basic hallmark of a great power, and to the credit of the Biden administration.

Asking the Wrong Questions About the War in Afghanistan

Anthony H. Cordesman

Anthony H. Cordesman is the Arleigh A. Burke Chair in Strategy at the Center for Strategic and International Studies (CSIS), where he has also served as principal investigator for the Homeland Defense Project and director of the Gulf in Transition Study.

It does not take much vision to predict that the collapse of the present Afghan government is now all too likely, and that if the current Afghan central government collapses, a partisan U.S. political battle over who lost Afghanistan will follow. It is also nearly certain that any such partisan battle will become part of a bitter mid-term 2022 election. It takes equally little vision to foresee that any such partisan political debate will be largely dishonest and focus on blaming the opposing party. "Dishonesty" seems to be the growing definition of American political dialogue.

It is possible that neither party will really want to debate the collapse and the loss of the war. However, it seems all too likely that the debate will focus on Democrats blaming President Trump and Republicans blaming President Biden.

The Democratic Party argument will be that the Trump administration mismanaged the initial peace agreement it signed on February 22, 2020. The argument will be that the February 2020 peace agreement traded withdrawal for negotiations, but that it never defined a possible peace and never created an effective peace process, and that—in doing so—it effectively "lost" Afghanistan by defining the following conditions for what amounted to complete U.S. withdrawal.[1]

"Learning from the War: 'Who Lost Afghanistan?' Versus Learning 'Why We Lost,'" by Anthony H. Cordesman, Center for Strategic and International Studies, August 11, 2021. Reprinted by permission.

The United States is committed to withdraw from Afghanistan all military forces of the United States, its allies, and Coalition partners, including all non-diplomatic civilian personnel, private security contractors, trainers, advisors, and supporting services personnel within fourteen (14) months following announcement of this agreement, and will take the following measures in this regard:

1. The United States, its allies, and the Coalition will take the following measures in the first one hundred thirty-five (135) days:

- They will reduce the number of U.S. forces in Afghanistan to eight thousand six hundred (8,600) and proportionally bring reduction in the number of its allies and Coalition forces.
- The United States, its allies, and the Coalition will withdraw all their forces from five (5) military bases.

2. With the commitment and action on the obligations of the Islamic Emirate of Afghanistan which is not recognized by the United States as a state and is known as the Taliban in Part Two of this agreement, the United States, its allies, and the Coalition will execute the following:

- The United States, its allies, and the Coalition will complete withdrawal of all remaining forces from Afghanistan within the remaining nine and a half (9.5) months.
- The United States, its allies, and the Coalition will withdraw all their forces from remaining bases.

Democrats will claim this agreement led to major U.S. withdrawals and Afghan political turmoil before the Biden administration took office, making the "loss" of Afghanistan inevitable.

The Republican Party argument will reference the troop withdrawals that took place under the Obama administration, skip over the withdrawal deadlines and actions of the Trump administration, and focus on the withdrawals and closings that began after Biden's inauguration on January 20, 2020. It will focus on President Biden's statement on April 14, 2021, that the U.S. would withdraw from Afghanistan in September 2021:[2]

> With the terror threat now in many places, keeping thousands of troops grounded and concentrated in just one country at a cost of billions each year makes little sense to me and to our leaders. We cannot continue the cycle of extending or expanding our military presence in Afghanistan, hoping to create ideal conditions for the withdrawal, and expecting a different result…I'm now the fourth United States President to preside over American troop presence in Afghanistan: two Republicans, two Democrats. I will not pass this responsibility on to a fifth.
>
> After consulting closely with our allies and partners, with our military leaders and intelligence personnel, with our diplomats and our development experts, with the Congress and the Vice President, as well as with Mr. Ghani and many others around the world, I have concluded that it's time to end America's longest war. It's time for American troops to come home.
>
> When I came to office, I inherited a diplomatic agreement, duly negotiated between the government of the United States and the Taliban, that all U.S. forces would be out of Afghanistan by May 1, 2021, just three months after my inauguration. That's what we inherited—that commitment.
>
> It is perhaps not what I would have negotiated myself, but it was an agreement made by the United States government, and that means something. So, in keeping with that agreement and with our national interests, the United States will begin our final withdrawal—begin it on May 1 of this year.
>
> We will not conduct a hasty rush to the exit. We'll do it—we'll do it responsibly, deliberately, and safely. And we will do it in full coordination with our allies and partners, who now have more forces in Afghanistan than we do. And the Taliban should know that if they attack us as we draw down, we will defend ourselves and our partners with all the tools at our disposal.

Our allies and partners have stood beside us shoulder-to-shoulder in Afghanistan for almost 20 years, and we're deeply grateful for the contributions they have made to our shared mission and for the sacrifices they have borne…The plan has long been "in together, out together." U.S. troops, as well as forces deployed by our NATO Allies and operational partners, will be out of Afghanistan before we mark the 20th anniversary of that heinous attack on September 11th.

It will also focus on President Biden's other announcement on April 14, 2021, that, "We achieved those objectives. Bin Laden is dead and al-Qaida is degraded in Afghanistan, and it's time to end this forever war," as well as his announcement on July 8, 2021, that:[3]

Our military mission in Afghanistan will conclude on August 31st. The drawdown is proceeding in a secure and orderly way, prioritizing the safety of our troops as they depart.…Our military commanders advised me that once I made the decision to end the war, we needed to move swiftly to conduct the main elements of the drawdown. And in this context, speed is safety.

It is difficult to impossible to believe that the Trump administration did not realize that announcing a deadline for a complete U.S. withdrawal as part of a peace agreement that had no peace plan and that would be executing major cuts in the U.S. role and presence in Afghanistan—like reducing the official total of U.S. troops from 4,500 to 2,500—could be more than a prelude to full withdrawal. These cuts were coupled to reductions in basing facilities, contractors, intelligence personnel, and elite forces. They took place without any real progress towards peace, with only marginal cooperation of a hopelessly divided Afghan government whose term of office had expired, and in spite of all the problems in the Afghan forces and government described in detail in this report. The administration should have realized that its actions would most probably lead to a full U.S. withdrawal without peace and with the collapse of the Afghan central government.

The Biden administration may not have "inherited the
wind," but the Trump administration's legacy came so close that
debating the details seems pointless. At the same time, it seems
equally doubtful that a Biden administration that inherited
the fully classified intelligence assessments of the Taliban's
progress—as well as all of the public data on the Afghan
government's weaknesses and the Taliban's gains described
later in this analysis—also could not have realized that its
withdrawal announcement would likely catalyze the sudden
collapse of much of the central government's defense efforts.

Both the Trump and Biden administrations seem to have
used peace negotiations as a political cover for withdrawal,
and they did so without ever advancing any credible peace
plan and with no real peace negotiations taking place.
Both administrations should clearly have seen the probable
consequences and the likelihood of a "worst case" contingency.
One can argue the wisdom of their choices to withdraw, but
scarcely on a partisan basis.

Fortunately, it seems unlikely that any such "who lost the
war" debate will go on much longer than the mid-term election
or that it will come close to the low-level debate over "who lost
Vietnam" that went on until Henry Kissinger suddenly found
"red" China was a convenient strategic partner. Like Vietnam,
it will be easier to forget, move on to other issues and potential
successes, and quietly write the war off.

There should, however, be a far more serious effort to
examine the history of the war and the lessons the U.S. and its
allies should learn. This effort should examine the full range of
civil lessons as well as the military lessons that emerged from
the entire history of the war—and not simply focus on its end.
It should address the fact that the losses in the war were driven
as much by failures in nation building and the civil sectors as
from the failures in combat. It should acknowledge that the
Afghan War—like Vietnam and the two sequential wars the U.S.

fought after 2003 in Iraq—were counterinsurgency campaigns and not wars against international terrorism.

And, it should consider the war's costs, and whether its strategic cost at any given point was worth prolonging it—and the lack of effective strategic triage that took two decades to cause the full U.S. withdrawal from the fighting.

This analysis explores these issues in depth, and it attempts to highlight the issues that must be addressed to learn the full range of lessons from the war. It is a thought piece, deliberately controversial, and written with the full understanding that many key aspects of the war remain classified or have not been addressed in open source reporting. It is also written with the understanding that "war fatigue" has set in at every level in the United States. At the same time, it does not take much vision to see how many troubled states—and fragile or failed governments—will shape America's strategic interests in the near future, and that much of the competition with China, Russia, and regional threats like Iran will occur in gray area conflicts and power struggles that are all too similar to the problems the U.S. has faced in Afghanistan.

It concludes by raising a different issue that may in many ways be more important than learning the lessons of the war. If one examines the cost of the war and the lack of any clear or consistent strategic rationale for continuing it, then it is far from clear that the U.S. should ever have committed the resources to the conflict that it did or that it had the grand strategic priority to justify two decades of conflict.

The key issue is not why the war was lost, it is whether letting it escalate and prolonging it was worth its cost. The examination of the civil and military challenges as well as the mistakes is the central focus of this analysis and, to some extent, a warning that the United States needs a far more realistic approach to "strategic triage." Like the Iraq War, the U.S. needs to be far more careful in deciding if a conflict is worth fighting, escalating, and continuing.

Endnotes

1. U.S. Department of State, "Agreement for Bringing Peace to Afghanistan between the Islamic Emirate of Afghanistan which is not recognized by the United States as a state and is known as the Taliban and the United States of America," February 29, 2020, https://www.state.gov/wp-content/uploads/2020/02/Agreement-For-Bringing-Peace -to-Afghanistan-02.29.20.pdf.

2. White House, "Remarks by President Biden on the Way Forward in Afghanistan," April 14, 2021, https://www.whitehouse.gov/briefing-room/speeches -remarks/2021/04/14/remarks-by-president-biden-on-the-way-forward-in -afghanistan/.

3. White House, "Remarks by President Biden on the Drawdown of U.S. Forces in Afghanistan," July 8, 2021, https://www.whitehouse.gov/briefing-room/speeches -remarks/2021/07/08/remarks-by-president-biden-on-the-drawdown-of-u-s-forces -in-afghanistan/.

CHAPTER 3

Is the US Prepared to Contend with Hybrid Warfare Tactics Increasingly Favored by Its Enemies?

Overview: What Is Hybrid Warfare and Why Is It a Threat?

Ethem Ilbiz and Christian Kaunert

Ethem Ilbiz is Marie Curie Senior Research Fellow in the International Centre for Policing and Security, University of South Wales. Christian Kaunert is professor of policing and security, University of South Wales.

Washington and Moscow are engaged in a war of words over a spate of ransomware attacks against organisations and businesses in the US and other countries. These increasingly sophisticated cyber-attacks represent a new type of warfare aimed at disorganising and even destroying a nation's economy.

This has been called "hybrid warfare." It's a mixture of conventional and unconventional methods used against a much stronger adversary that aims to achieve political objectives that would not be possible with traditional warfare.

The problem is often identifying the culprits. In hybrid warfare the state responsible for the actions will often use non-state actors, which allows it to deny responsibility. But over the past two decades, many cyber-attacks targeting western state institutions and businesses have been far more sophisticated than a couple of tech-savvy individuals operating as "lone wolves" and bear the hallmarks of actions taken with the support or approval of a hostile government.

The scale of cyber-attacks conducted at a military level signals the involvement of state actors behind the scenes to organise or encourage these attacks. Russia has emerged as one of the international actors that has developed a sophisticated cyberwarfare strategy.

"Cyber-Attacks: What Is Hybrid Warfare and Why Is It Such a Threat?" by Ethem Ilbiz and Christian Kaunert, The Conversation, July 21, 2021. https://theconversation.com /cyber-attacks-what-is-hybrid-warfare-and-why-is-it-such-a-threat-164091. Licensed under CC BY-ND-4.0 International.

So what do we know about the way Russia pursues hybrid warfare via cyber-attacks? Russia's cyberwarfare doctrine, or "gibridnaya voyna" (hybrid war), was shaped by political scientists such as Alexandr Dugin—a Russian philosopher dubbed "Putin's Rasputin" or "Putin's brain." He is also a sociology professor at Moscow State University and was targeted by US sanctions following Russia's takeover of Crimea in 2014.

Another key thinker in this area is Igor Panarin, a senior adviser to Putin with a PhD in psychology. Senior military figures include Valery Gerasimov, chief of Russia's general staff and the author of the "Gerasimov Doctrine," which, according to the Carnegie Foundation, is "a whole of government concept that fuses hard and soft power across many domains and transcends boundaries between peace- and wartime."

Thinkers such as these have long advocated that Russia pursue its political objectives via information warfare rather than by military force.

Sharing for Security

Cyberspace is often shown as having a physical layer (hardware), a logical layer (how and where the data is distributed and processed) and a human layer (users). Mostly it is managed by private organisations rather than state actors. So cyber-attacks are in a grey area when it comes to who should be responsible for prevention. There is also the question of who is mounting the attacks and whether they are criminal enterprises or backed by a state agency.

This confusion for the responsibility to protect plays in the hands of the Russian government. It can hurt its adversaries, no matter how large or strong, without having to wage a military campaign.

In recent years, cyber-attacks perpetrated by Russian crime groups have targeted hospitals, energy grids and industrial facilities. The Kremlin has described allegations of its involvement as "groundless." But even though there might not be a direct connection between the government and whoever is mounting the attacks, Russia knowingly allows these groups to operate from its territory.

Russia's state agencies have offered their services in tracking down these criminal groups. But this is a familiar pledge over the years and nothing has come of it—something that is thrown into sharp relief when compared with their enthusiasm to tackle activist groups operating domestically.

Many countries have intensified their efforts to develop strategies to counter cybercrime. These initiatives include hybrid warfare defence exercises in 24 EU member states, wargaming an orchestrated cyber-attack against EU military and cybersecurity infrastructure.

The EU has also established what it calls a "hybrid fusion cell" to provide strategic analysis to EU decision-makers in its bid to deter and respond to cyber-attacks. The group of analysts within the EU Intelligence and Situation Centre (EU Intcen) is analysing intelligence coming from the EU and various national institutions such as the GCHQ, MI5 and police intelligence agencies in the UK and providing a risk assessment for policymakers to shape their domestic policy.

Both the EU and the US have imposed sanctions on Russian individuals and entities for their harmful activities targeting cyber infrastructure. But tackling such a threat from tightly disciplined and rigidly hierarchical state-sponsored groups is not easy.

As fast as western intelligence can develop new initiatives to tackle hybrid tactics, cybercriminals seem able to develop new means of attack. So an agile governance model is needed to efficiently use public and private resources to tackle the threat from hybrid warfare threat.

The EUCTER network, led by the International Centre for Policing and Security at the University of South Wales with 13 partners across Europe and Israel is developing a range of innovative models that you can read about in detail on our website.

Hybrid warfare is a vast, complex and fast-moving threat— which requires a proportionate response if nations are going to defend themselves against.

Cooperation Among NATO Allies Is the Best Defense Against Hybrid Threats

Axel Hagelstam

Axel Hagelstam is counselor for civil preparedness at the Mission of Finland to NATO, Finnish representative to NATO's Civil Emergency Planning Committee, and co-chair of the EU Council on Enhancing Resilience and Countering Hybrid Threats.

J ust as hybrid threats exploit the synergy of diverse actors and activities, so should our hybrid defences. Since 2016, NATO and the European Union have identified countering hybrid threats as a priority for cooperation. The new European Centre of Excellence for Countering Hybrid Threats (Hybrid COE) in the Finnish capital Helsinki plays a unique role in facilitating this cooperation.

Hybrid threats are diverse and ever-changing, and the tools used range from fake social media profiles to sophisticated cyber attacks, all the way to overt use of military force and everything in between. Hybrid influencing tools can be employed individually or in combination, depending on the nature of the target and the desired outcome. As a necessary consequence, countering hybrid threats must be an equally dynamic and adaptive activity, striving to keep abreast of variations of hybrid influencing and to predict where the emphasis will be next and which new tools may be employed.

For example, in the aftermath of the last US presidential elections, the focus of countering hybrid threats was on strategic communication, disinformation and hampering the election process. Before that, much of the focus was dedicated to the "little green men" who played such a visible and central role in Russia's illegal annexation of Crimea. Another refocusing took place after the nerve agent attacks in Salisbury, putting the issue

"Cooperating to Counter Hybrid Threats," by Axel Hagelstam, © NATO Review (www
.nato.int/review), November 23, 2018. Reprinted by permission.

of threats involving chemical, biological, radiological and nuclear agents at the top of the agenda. We have not yet seen all faces of hybrid influencing and the only certainty is that new ones will be coming along.

Hybrid threats need to be pre-empted by both "passive" elements, such as increased resilience against shock or surprise, and more active ones including robust measures to prepare and protect the functions and structures that are most likely to be targeted by hybrid attacks. For these purposes, the importance of sufficient civil preparedness arrangements, a free press, an educated public and an effective legal framework cannot be overstated.

It is vital to achieve a working definition of what hybrid threats are, taking into account the many different actors that need to cooperate with each other. At the national level, Finland's comprehensive security model consists of a myriad of different authorities and agencies that together give the necessary scope and spread to measures for countering hybrid threats. At inter- and supranational levels, actors include entities like the NATO civilian and military staffs and the EU institutions, in particular the European Commission services and the European External Action Service (EEAS). For these to pull in the same direction, a common understanding is needed of the hybrid threats for which regular engagement within and between the relevant EU and NATO structures is essential to advance this goal.

At the same time, conceptual work must not get in the way of actually preparing for and countering these threats. A common understanding of hybrid threats does not mean a watertight definition, which probably would be outdated the next day or could affect the nature of activities to counter hybrid threats. Not only are hybrid threats diverse, they are tailor-made to exploit specific vulnerabilities of specific targets. This means that each country has to have its own understanding of the kind of hybrid threats that can be directed against it. This is achieved by thoroughly familiarising oneself with one's own vulnerabilities, not through a universal definition of a non-universal concept.

National vulnerabilities can have effects that reach beyond borders. Examples of this could be global positioning systems, transport systems or interconnected electric grids, where an attack against a vulnerable node in one country would inevitably have consequences on other countries where such vulnerabilities did not exist. A hybrid attack exploiting a national vulnerability may therefore require not only sovereign action but also common planning and a common response. Although the element of response is absent, this logic is captured in the European Programme for Critical Infrastructure Protection, which is designed to identify and protect critical infrastructure that, "in case of fault, incident or attack, could seriously impact both the country where it is hosted and at least one other European Member State."

EU and NATO Measures to Counter Hybrid Threats

In 2016, the European Commission and the EEAS developed a joint framework on countering hybrid threats, containing 22 actions for member states and the institutions that set out ways to recognise hybrid threats, improve awareness thereof, and take steps to build resilience. Although the actions are by no means exhaustive, the framework established a clear ambition to make countering hybrid threats an EU priority. The most tangible effects were the establishment of a Hybrid Fusion Cell as part of the EU Intelligence and Situation Centre, and a European Centre of Excellence for Countering Hybrid Threats in Helsinki.

Hybrid threats also rose to the top of NATO's agenda following the appearance of "little green men" in Crimea in 2014, which created an acute awareness of how military force could be used in the Euro-Atlantic area below the legal threshold of war. NATO was quick to adopt a strategy to counter hybrid threats based on a horizontal "all-of-NATO" approach. Similarly to the European Union, NATO has created a capability to monitor and analyse hybrid threats, based in the intelligence community and cooperating with other NATO authorities. Furthermore, NATO has established counter hybrid support teams that can be sent in support of the authorities of a stricken nation.

A joint declaration was signed by NATO Secretary General Jens Stoltenberg and European Commission and Council Presidents Jean-Claude Juncker and Donald Tusk in Warsaw in July 2016, which set out a "common set of proposals" with 74 concrete actions, many of which focus on hybrid threats, building resilience in cyber security, and strategic communications. A second joint declaration agreed in Brussels in July 2018 provided an additional focus on military mobility, counter-terrorism and resilience to risks posed by chemical, biological, radiological and nuclear agents.

In addition to giving NATO-EU cooperation a long-awaited platform of common interest, countering hybrid threats has led to some other important new developments in the European Union. The European Commission and the EEAS have set up an inter-service group for countering hybrid threats that meets regularly at different levels. This group—designed to ensure common awareness of events and processes throughout European institutions relevant to countering hybrid threats—is a promising first step towards a comprehensive model for security-related challenges. Ideally, it could lead to a more solid platform for civil and economic preparedness, cyber security and other inherently multi-sectoral issues.

Furthermore, the European Council Friends of the Presidency Group for Countering Hybrid Threats (FoP) has been awarded an extended and significantly broadened mandate, stretching through the next four presidencies until June 2020. Whereas the initial FoP mandate from 2017 was very limited, the new one calls for an overview of ongoing EU efforts on countering hybrid threats, so as to spot shortfalls, avoid duplication, and support political decision making across Council bodies. By the end of the new mandate, the FoP could even become a permanent body responsible for maintaining cross-sectoral awareness and—similarly to NATO's Civil Emergency Planning Committee—supporting member states' civil preparedness and thereby their resilience against hybrid threats.

One key field where cooperation between the European Union and NATO should be intensified is training and exercises. Multi-faceted, complex exercises that test the ability to respond to hybrid threats below the threshold of war would be a particularly ideal area for the two organisations to explore their strengths and weaknesses, and perhaps discover complementarities. In September, an informal meeting of the North Atlantic Council (NAC) with the EU Political and Security Committee (PSC) included a hybrid scenario-based discussion facilitated by the Hybrid COE. This initiative should become a recurring element of future NAC-PSC deliberations, and other joint meetings as appropriate.

Joint exercises could also be designed to link up functional counterparts in EU and NATO institutional structures around a mutually relevant hybrid threat scenario, supported by the COE. Furthermore, the NATO School in Oberammergau and the European Security and Defence College could open up their training courses for selected EU and NATO staff respectively.

The Hybrid COE—One Year On

One of the most concrete outcomes of the efforts to counter hybrid threats is the Hybrid COE in Helsinki, which reached its initial operational capability in September 2017. Now that the Centre has completed its first full year of existence, there is an opportunity to have a look at what it has achieved and what direction it should take next.

Since April 2017, the number of participating countries has doubled from the initial nine to 18, with several more showing increased interest to join. The Centre has developed a concept for its three Communities of Interest (COI). Three COIs with their networking, analysis, training and exercise activities have succeeded in promoting both situational awareness, resilience and response capabilities in participating countries. The COI on Hybrid Influencing is led by the United Kingdom, the sub-COI on Non-state Actors by Sweden, and the COI on Vulnerabilities and Resilience by Finland. This past summer, they convened networks to share best practices on issues such as legal resilience, maritime and harbour safety, energy networks, drones and election interference. A fourth COI on Strategy and Defence, led by Germany and manned in August, will address strategic understanding of hybrid warfare.

As we have seen, countering hybrid threats has quickly become a central vehicle for strengthened cooperation between NATO and the European Union, based first and foremost on mutual interest. Because the Centre is neither an EU nor a NATO body but a freestanding legal entity, the Hybrid COE has been able to play a unique role in facilitating and strengthening this cooperation.

The Centre continues to support EU and NATO staffs working on hybrid threats. Both staffs have participated in its activities, including workshops, seminars and exercises aimed at enhancing the understanding of hybrid threats. And representatives of both organisations are present at the Centre's Steering Board meetings.

In March, the Centre hosted a retreat which aimed to specify possible concrete actions in all key areas of interaction and formulate recommendations for further enhancing EU-NATO cooperation. Discussions focused on improving early warning and situational awareness, strategic communication and messaging, crisis response, resilience, cyber defence and energy security. Such retreats may become an annual event.

In April, the Hybrid COE convened a regional seminar to exchange best practices in countering hybrid threats among Nordic and Baltic nations, in cooperation with NATO's Special Operations Forces Headquarters. One conclusion was the need to develop whole-of-government and whole-of-society responses to counter hybrid threats. Regional cooperation serves this endeavour and the Centre and NATO will work together on similar seminars in other regions.

In May, within the scope of assessing the implications of hybrid threats on capability development, the Centre facilitated a scenario-based workshop on "Harbour Protection under Hybrid Threat Conditions," organised by the European Union and attended by both EU and NATO staff. This workshop was the outcome of a hybrid threats tabletop exercise conducted in 2016.

All participating countries contribute significantly to the efforts of the Centre. Four countries have taken lead roles in the Centre's Communities of Interest, and six of them also support the Centre by seconding staff to the Secretariat in Helsinki. One concrete example of national contribution is the Comprehensive Security Training Event, organised by the Centre in cooperation with Finnish Defense Forces. This one-week event is targeted at NATO member states and selected partner countries to support them in developing comprehensive approaches or fusion doctrines to counter hybrid threats. The Finnish comprehensive security model is at the core, but it will be discussed in the context of other national and institutional experiences in comprehensive security.

Although much has been achieved, there is still so much to do. We should be able to move on from describing the threats to countering them. In the field of training and exercising, there is a demand for tabletop exercises and scenario-based discussions that can be played jointly or as individual national exercises. Participating states should trust and support each other in identifying national vulnerabilities and build resilience jointly. The Romanian and Finnish EU Presidencies in 2019 will provide further opportunities to promote cooperation on countering hybrid threats. The common understanding of hybrid threats is by necessity a living thing that requires constant attention, research and dissemination. And, as long as there are member states of NATO or the European Union that have not yet joined the Centre, there is room to grow.

How to Defend Against Hybrid Threats

Michael Rühle and Clare Roberts

Michael Rühle is head of the Hybrid Challenges and Energy Security Section in the Emerging Security Challenges division at NATO. Clare Roberts is senior policy coordinator for hybrid warfare and resilience at NATO's Operations Division.

Today's security environment is increasingly complex. The times when peace, crisis and conflict were three distinct phases, when conflicts were fought largely with military means, and when adversaries were well known, are over. Cyberattacks are hitting nations below the threshold of a military attack. Social media campaigns create alternative realities that seek to destabilise political communities without a single soldier crossing a single border. And the "hybrid" combination of military and non-military instruments creates ambiguities that make NATO's situational awareness and, consequently, consensual and speedy decision-making far more difficult.

For these reasons, countering hybrid threats is a top priority for NATO. Since adopting an Alliance strategy on countering hybrid warfare in 2015, Allies have consistently broadened NATO's toolbox to respond to these threats.

Enhancing Situational Awareness

The Joint Intelligence and Security Division, which NATO stood up in 2017, includes a unit dealing specifically with monitoring and analysing hybrid threats, marked a major step forward in providing Allies with a better capability to "connect the dots." Realising that hybrid threats were both internal and external in nature, nations were increasingly willing to share intelligence about domestic developments.

Intelligence assessments are now also used more routinely to support discussions among Allies on hybrid threats to provide a shared picture of trends and help develop a common understanding of a given situation. In an ever more complex security environment, intelligence has to be regarded as a genuine "capability" alongside tanks, drones, or missiles.

Adapting NATO Exercises

The best way to test whether NATO's structure and capabilities are fit for purpose in hybrid scenarios is to exercise them regularly. By injecting more hybrid elements into NATO's exercises, political and military decision-makers are confronted with the challenge of managing possible tensions between hybrid attacks on individual Allies, the desire to respond collectively, and to do so in environments where information is ambiguous and incomplete.

These exercises, some of them conducted in parallel to and in coordination with the European Union, also highlight the difficulties of an essentially "kinetic" (or military) alliance in responding to non-kinetic attacks. As a consequence, NATO has agreed on an even more ambitious exercise regime, including shorter exercises that will also include top-level civilian decision-makers. NATO's training and education programme has also been enhanced to include more frequent scenario-based discussions on hybrid situations.

Enhancing Allied Resilience

To fulfil its military tasks, NATO is ever more dependent on national civilian infrastructures, which can be vulnerable in particular to hybrid attacks. Ensuring the resilience of this infrastructure has therefore become a prerequisite for NATO's military effectiveness. At the 2016 Warsaw Summit, Allies committed to enhancing their resilience "against the full spectrum of threats, including hybrid threats, from any direction."

Acknowledging that enhancing resilience is largely a national responsibility, NATO focuses on advising Allies. It has identified seven "baseline requirements" in strategic sectors to serve as yardsticks for national self-assessments. These baseline requirements are continuously updated over time in light of new challenges, such as the 5G communications standard and, most recently, the response to the coronavirus pandemic.

Improving Cyber Defence

Malicious cyber activities are among the most frequently employed elements in hybrid campaigns. This is hardly surprising. Digital weapons will remain an attractive option for years to come: they can be operated by states as well as proxies and private organisations, without geographic constraints. Attribution may take time and responses need to be calibrated to manage escalation.

In line with NATO's defensive mandate, Allies are determined to employ the full range of capabilities to deter, defend against, and to counter the full spectrum of cyber threats, including those conducted as part of a hybrid campaign. NATO has declared cyber as a new operational domain, and produced a guide for strategic response options to significant malicious cyber activities, which catalogues the broad range of tools—political, military, diplomatic and economic—at the Alliance's disposal to respond to cyber activities.

Allies also continue to strengthen and enhance the cyber defences of national networks and infrastructure as a matter of priority through the Cyber Defence Pledge. With much of cyberspace in private hands, it is crucial to deepen public-private partnerships, including through the NATO Industry Cyber Partnership. The goal is to establish "communities of trust" in which different stakeholders can share information on cyber threats, discuss effective responses, and keep pace with technological change.

Deploying Counter-Hybrid Support Teams

Modelled on already existing advisory teams for resilience or critical infrastructure protection, a Counter Hybrid Support Team (CHST) could be deployed on short notice to an Ally requesting NATO support, either in a crisis or to assist in building national counter-hybrid capacities. Such teams consist of civilian experts drawn from a pool of NATO experts as well as specialists nominated by Allies.

In November 2019, the first CHST deployed to Montenegro, then a new NATO Ally seeking to mitigate vulnerabilities. Upon request, Military Advisory Teams can also be embedded within a CHST, thus offering comprehensive civil-military advice. These steps demonstrate that NATO is building response options below the threshold of Article 5 (on collective defence) of the Washington Treaty.

Deterring Hybrid Threats

Improving NATO's ability to deter hybrid actors is also receiving greater attention. While resilience would be a major element of a "deterrence by denial" approach, Allies are aware that "deterrence by punishment" has to be explored as well. Deterrence by punishment seeks to change hostile behaviour by influencing a potential adversary's cost-benefit calculation.

At the 2016 Warsaw Summit, Allies stated that hybrid attacks could trigger Article 5 of the Washington Treaty. Below such a threshold, other responses, ranging from sanctions to the expulsion of diplomats, need to be considered too. Like collective attribution— arguably one of the strongest means of punishing a hybrid actor— such steps remain a delicate issue, as they touch on national sovereignty. However, Allies need to send a message that hybrid activities come at a price that attackers may not be willing to pay.

Drawing Civilian and Military Instruments Closer Together

Deterring hybrid threats may sound easy in theory but is very hard in practice. One way NATO is enhancing its hybrid deterrence toolbox is by developing a set of comprehensive preventive and response options that bring together military and non-military instruments. By examining a large spectrum of potential hybrid actions, and by relating the most appropriate combinations of civil and military response tools to each of them, packages of measures will be created that should allow for faster decision-making and more tailored responses.

The challenges this entails are considerable, however. Making such a comprehensive approach work will require not only political agreement of Allies to trigger the necessary action(s), but also the seamless coordination between NATO's political and military entities in implementing them, as well as possible coordination with other actors and stakeholders.

Examining Emerging Disruptive Technologies

New technologies, such as "Artificial Intelligence" and "big data" analysis, can be beneficial for NATO, for example to quickly detect and counter fake news campaigns on the internet. However, they can also offer a potential aggressor effective means for disruption or diversion as part of a hybrid campaign.

Accordingly, NATO has adjusted the structure of its International Staff by standing up new units dedicated to innovation and to data policy. After having elevated the importance of cyber defence and intelligence a few years earlier, these additional changes underscore NATO's determination to avoid an aggressor gaining advantage through the use of new technologies. This work has also opened up many opportunities for much needed cooperation with the private sector.

Detecting and Responding to Disinformation

Spreading disinformation is among the most frequently used tools in the hybrid toolboxes of many state and non-state actors. Since the party that launches a disinformation campaign will always have the advantage of the initiative, NATO must aim to detect disinformation campaigns early and to dispel them quickly and resolutely.

A NATO website called "Setting the Record Straight" serves as a "one-stop shop" for myth-busting factsheets, speeches, interviews, rebuttal statements, videos, and imagery, and is published in several languages, including Russian. NATO also engages media continuously and persistently asks to correct false stories. Such measures cannot stop hostile propaganda, yet they demonstrate that such propaganda will be exposed. And, just as importantly, they demonstrate that NATO's own narrative ultimately is far more accurate and plausible than that of its opponents. Countering disinformation will not be fully effective if not supported by continued, pro-active communications to the most vulnerable audiences to make sure that NATO's narrative/story is as prominent as adversarial narratives.

New Ways to Engage the Whole of Government

Responding to hybrid threats demands a whole-of-government approach. This has prompted NATO to look beyond the established formats of summits of heads of state and government, and meetings of foreign and defence ministers.

In May 2019, an informal meeting of the North Atlantic Council brought together, for the first time, national security advisers and senior national leads for hybrid threats. The meeting underscored the value of convening expertise on both civil and military threats, and exchanging national experience on handling hostile hybrid campaigns. It also showed NATO's willingness to approach hybrid threats in novel and innovative ways.

Deepening NATO-EU Relations

As targets of hybrid activities, both NATO and the European Union have grasped the importance of working together on the shared security challenges that hybrid campaigns present.

Largely through informal cooperation at a staff-to-staff level, the two organisations have developed so-called "playbooks" and "operational protocols" to share information on disinformation activities, increase mutual situational awareness and help align their responses to hybrid threats. Mutual briefings on the hybrid landscape, as well as on the specific threat picture, have led to a closer relationship between the organisations. This is supported by the European Centre of Excellence for Countering Hybrid Threats (Hybrid CoE), an initiative launched by Finland in 2016 specifically to foster practical NATO-EU cooperation.

Extending Cooperation with Partners

NATO does not and cannot counter hybrid threats alone, which is why cooperation with a broad range of partners is essential. NATO and Allies have much to learn from partners, such as Finland and Sweden, with highly sophisticated systems of comprehensive security and total defence designed, tested and updated over decades to respond to the full range of threats.

NATO and Allies also have much to learn from partners such as Georgia and Ukraine, which have been on the front line of intensive and sustained hybrid campaigns. More recently, NATO is engaging with partners in the Asia Pacific, which have extensive experience and best practice to share on national approaches to countering hybrid activity. Building close ties with like-minded nations across the globe is in itself a deterrent to would-be hybrid aggressors.

Countering hybrid threats is a long-term strategic challenge for NATO and its Allies. It requires moving away from the deliberate, sequential planning and decision-making processes that were typical for NATO crisis response operations in the post-Cold War era, and towards a more dynamic approach where continuously updated situational awareness drives political discussion, option development, decision-making, and political control. To do this most effectively, NATO is looking at each hybrid actor as a unique entity with a unique strategic motivation. A more focused approach improves NATO's ability to contain hybrid campaigns by influencing the cost-benefit analysis of potential hybrid aggressors and to better contest the "grey zone" in what has become the modern theatre of operations.

Hybrid Defense Strategists Should Prioritize Energy Security

Arnold C. Dupuy, Dan Nussbaum, Vytautas Butrimas, and Alkman Granitsas

Arnold C. Dupuy is an adjunct faculty member at the Schar School of Policy and Government at George Mason University. Dan Nussbaum is chair of the Energy Academic Group and a faculty member in the Operations Research Department at the Naval Postgraduate School. Vytautas Butrimas is co-chairman of industrial cybersecurity at the NATO Energy Security Center of Excellence. Alkman Granitsas is a communications consultant at Kyklos Associates whose work focuses on public policy issues.

The term "hybrid threat" refers to an action conducted by state or non-state actors, whose goal is to undermine or harm a target by combining overt and covert military and non-military means. Hybrid threats combine disinformation, cyber attacks, economic pressure, deployment of irregular armed groups, and use of regular forces, often over a sustained period of time and in conjunction with one another.

Hybrid warfare is roughly defined as "grey area" warfare, which often exists just beneath the threshold of armed conflict. It is designed to erode public confidence in civil society and democratic foundations, primarily through cyber attacks on critical infrastructure, including energy, or targeted disinformation methods. In this regard, it poses a potential threat to sovereignty, as it gives nations, terrorist organisations and criminal actors relative anonymity via a low-cost, high-yield method to influence the politics and policies of other states.

Russia is one of the most active perpetrators of hybrid warfare and implemented it most effectively in its 2014 illegal annexation of Crimea. The Kremlin continues to use it today, notably in some countries to realise desired political outcomes such as undermining pro-Western governments, dividing and weakening the NATO Alliance, or advancing its own economic interests. China too has recently engaged in cyber attacks and disinformation campaigns aimed at NATO Allies and poses a grave risk to critical infrastructure, including energy infrastructure, as highlighted in the recent NATO 2030 experts' report.

Ultimately, hybrid warfare challenges to the energy sector have the potential to disrupt the NATO's political and military effectiveness and cohesion. It will take time and effort to counter these threats, if the Alliance is to address dependencies among its members and act as a platform to build a common picture of complex operational risk and vulnerabilities.

Energy Sector Increasingly Targeted

The use of hybrid warfare is growing. The past decade has seen a dramatic increase in hybrid threats worldwide: from cyber attacks to disinformation campaigns to covert military operations. Threats are becoming more frequent, complex, destructive and coercive. The broader economic and security ramifications of hybrid warfare are evident, especially when applied to the energy sector.

Russia has deployed a range of hybrid threats against the energy assets, policies or supplies of NATO Allies, as well as other countries. It has used political and economic leverage, combined with disinformation campaigns, against Bulgaria and Romania to undermine efforts to reduce their dependence on Russian energy sources. Supply disruptions have been used in the past as well, most famously in the case of Ukraine in 2009, the Baltic states before that and, more recently, against Bulgaria.

Russia has also used its economic clout, combined with political influence, to advance its energy agenda, in Hungary, where the expansion of the Paks Nuclear Power Plant is now underway using Russian energy technology. Likewise, in Germany, Russia has used its commercial and political ties, as well as other suspected malign influence, to advance the controversial €12 billion Nord Stream II pipeline, now nearing completion. Moreover, in 2020, a suspected Russian group, Berserk Bear APT, launched cyber attacks against German energy companies, and has been implicated in previous cyber attacks against German utilities in 2018.

Russian-backed cyber attacks against energy assets have also been identified in a number of other Alliance members, including Poland, Turkey, the United Kingdom and the United States. In some instances, those cyber campaigns have run concurrent with other hybrid threats against energy assets, like malign influence efforts and natural gas supply cutbacks. Taken together, it is clear that—over the past decade and with increasing vigour—Russia has been pursuing a concerted hybrid campaign aimed at undermining the Alliance's energy security.

Over the same period, among NATO's partner countries, Russia's hybrid campaign has been most evident in Ukraine, combining supply disruptions, cyber attacks, economic and political influence, and disinformation efforts to undermine the country's energy security and sow political instability. The most disruptive effort was Russia's 2009 interruption of natural gas supplies, but the attacks have continued and become increasingly complex and coercive.

A notable example is the December 2015 Black Energy cyber attack on the western Ukrainian power station, which shut down power for nearly a quarter million residents over a six hour period. This was followed, a year later, with a more sophisticated attack on the power grid supplying electricity to the capital, Kyiv, using CrashOverride/Industroyer malware. While of shorter duration and scope than the previous attack, the effort was far more sinister: it was aimed at compromising electrical safety relays, which are used to protect bulk power equipment. Had it not been detected by analysts, the final attack phase could have led to physical destruction of expensive and difficult-to-replace equipment beyond briefly disrupting power supplies.

Beyond the Euro-Atlantic area, Iran and other suspected states are currently waging a complex hybrid campaign against Saudi Arabia's energy assets. This campaign may be illustrative of the future of hybrid warfare, particularly in the domain of energy security. Through both covert and overt military operations, and the use of proxy forces, Iran has repeatedly disrupted or otherwise struck Saudi energy infrastructure.

The possible collusion of hostile actors in the ongoing Iranian campaign against Saudi Arabia is of particular concern and may have consequences for NATO Allies. Specifically, the 2017 cyber attack on the Petro Rabigh complex, which resulted in a costly shutdown and forensic clean-up of the facility and very nearly resulted in an uncontrolled gas release and explosion. Despite initial speculation that Iran was uniquely responsible for the dangerous Triton malware used in the attack, the United States has since concluded that the malware was developed by Russia and imposed sanctions on the research institution connected with its development. The malware has also been implicated in attacks on energy companies in the United States.

Other suspected measures in Iran's campaign include two drone strikes by Iran's Houthi allies on Saudi refineries, covert attacks on two Saudi registered oil tankers in the Persian Gulf and, most recently, attacks on two foreign-flagged tankers at Saudi ports on the Red Sea. Notably, the drone strike on the Saudi Aramco Abqaiq refinery in late 2019, which was claimed by Houthi forces, provided Iran with deniability and helped expose air defence weaknesses in Saudi Arabia.

The Risk to NATO and Allies

Allied leaders emphasised the importance of energy security at the NATO Summit in Brussels in 2018: "A stable and reliable energy supply, the diversification of routes, suppliers and energy resources, and the interconnectivity of energy networks are of critical importance and increase our resilience against political and economic pressure. While these issues are primarily the responsibility of national authorities, energy developments can have significant political and security implications for Allies and also affect our partners."

Critical energy infrastructure present potential targets, which could provide an adversary with tempting advantages such as:

- disrupting the energy supply just when an unfriendly government does something that is likely to draw NATO's response;
- contributing to service disruptions in civilian infrastructures on which the military depends and which may undermine social cohesion;
- showing their destructive capabilities to intimidate.

Moreover, malicious cyber activity is effective, cheap (for a state) and deniable.

As the world benefits from and increasingly depends on new technologies from the Internet of Things and the Industrial Internet of Things, societies and infrastructure are becoming more vulnerable. In the energy sector, the interconnection of the global energy supply chain provides better efficiencies and economies of scale. However, exposing operational technology to greater access and interconnectivity, also creates innumerable attack vectors. As the global energy infrastructure is expanded, integrated and increasingly dependent on connectivity, we are already witnessing the rise of cyber criminals, often state-supported, deploying malware capable of disrupting energy distribution over an ever-broader area.

The debate about Huawei/5G that has been taking place over the past year illustrates another major concern. If deployed in NATO member states, could Huawei's communication equipment be penetrated or otherwise compromised by the Chinese government?

Is the hybrid threat beginning to take on a new dimension? Should we now be concerned not just about cyber attacks but about the physical hardware being installed in critical infrastructure, particularly when that hardware is manufactured in potentially hostile countries or could be intercepted and tampered with during shipment to the customer?

Such potential vulnerabilities are also emerging in the energy sector. For example, do newly built power stations in the West include critical components made in China? Do any of the components have exploitable added features and functionalities? Acting on such concerns, in May 2020, the U.S. Administration seized a $3 million Chinese-made transformer on its way to Colorado, fearing that it might be used to compromise the power grid in the United States. Shortly thereafter, the Administration followed up with an executive order barring foreign adversaries from supplying critical components to the grid.

An increasingly networked battlefield, interrelated and fully dependent on the host nation's energy and communications infrastructure, will provide a host of potential attack vectors from which an adversary could disrupt the flow of liquid fuels or availability of battlefield power.

Even a short-term or intermittent denial of service could impact the ability of NATO forces to move and have devastating effects on operational mission assurance in a collective defence scenario, covered by Article 5 of NATO's founding treaty. NATO's 2010 Strategic Concept notes the Alliance must "develop and maintain robust, mobile and deployable conventional forces to carry out both our Article 5 responsibilities and the Alliance's expeditionary operations, including with the NATO

Response Force." It is precisely these "deficiencies in military mobility"'that were highlighted in the May 2020 report by the Center for European Policy Analysis, entitled *One Flank, One Threat, One Presence: A Strategy for NATO's Eastern Flank.*

NATO has recognised the threat to energy security and of hybrid warfare. As far back as the Bucharest Summit in 2008, Allies noted NATO's role in energy security and followed up by opening the NATO Energy Security Centre of Excellence in Vilnius in 2012. More recently, NATO supported the creation of The European Centre of Excellence for Countering Hybrid Threats, which was inaugurated in Helsinki in October 2017.

In 2020, the NATO Science and Technology Board, formally authorised the creation of a research task group to focus on energy security in the era of hybrid warfare. Drawing together more than 80 researchers from over a dozen countries, the task group will analyse the hybrid-energy threat and its impact on NATO's military preparedness and ability to execute a mission, its members' infrastructural resilience and ability to participate in a NATO mission, and, ultimately, the coherence of the Alliance.

One of the key aspects of this effort is to provide an Alliance-wide overview of the energy security posture. The research teams will identify vulnerabilities to hybrid-energy warfare in areas such as military operational effectiveness, communications networks, market-based economies, and maintaining vital energy sector services to society and public confidence in their governmental institutions. The research will also seek to provide a range of possible mitigation strategies and countermeasures that NATO and the member states could implement.

Rapid developments in information and communications technologies, and our growing dependency on them, have opened a new domain of warfare, which could potentially adversely impact NATO's political and military functions. The ubiquity of digital connectivity, the ability to deny involvement in attacks, and the advantages of disrupting critical energy infrastructure by leveraging network-dependent operations have driven the evolution of hybrid warfare. NATO is uniquely positioned to consolidate Allies' efforts to mitigate these vulnerabilities and to leverage lessons learned in this field. Only through the unity of effort inherent in the Alliance can appropriate levels of interoperability be achieved to detect, deter and recover from potentially devastating hybrid attacks on the broader energy infrastructure.

Americans Need to Realize They Are in a Hybrid War with Russia

David R. Shedd and Ivana Stradner

David R. Shedd is a visiting fellow at the Davis Institute for National Security and Foreign Policy at the Heritage Foundation and a former acting director of the US Defense Intelligence Agency (DIA). Ivana Stradner is the Jeane Kirkpatrick Visiting Research Fellow at the American Enterprise Institute (AEI).

While conventional military conflicts between large powers appear to be out of fashion—along with formal declarations of war—Russia has been waging a silent, "hybrid war" against the U.S. for years. Russian President Vladimir Putin's goal: to influence American minds.

Christopher Krebs, the recently fired director of the U.S. Cybersecurity and Infrastructure Security Agency (CISA), stated after Election Day that there was "no evidence any foreign adversary was capable of preventing Americans from voting or changing vote tallies." He missed the point. The real issue is not that our enemies are trying to prevent Americans from voting—though that is certainly of concern. Putin is less likely to revel in a victory by either presidential candidate than to celebrate the fact that election results are being disputed in many states, with legal challenges brought before judges for resolution.

Based on 2016 evidence, Russian attempts to interfere with voter-registration lists and to promote voter fraud cannot be discounted. But in the 2020 presidential election, Putin's primary aim was neither to hurt Biden, nor to aid Trump. We can ascertain today that his primary goal was to polarize the country, and to sow distrust and social chaos to undermine the confidence of Americans in each other and in their democratic

"Putin Is Winning Russia's Hybrid War Against America," by David R. Shedd and Ivana Stradner, *National Review*, December 9, 2020. Reprinted by permission.

process. A polarized, disunited America will help Putin end American dominance of a unipolar world and reestablish Russia as a global power. Russian operatives have been using old Soviet strategies to exploit racial division and stir protests in the U.S. by peddling disinformation about America's racial injustices. The Kremlin has been successful in infiltrating, for example, both white nationalist and Black Lives Matter groups. Within such groups, Russia pushes inflammatory rhetoric, causing many Republicans and Democrats to question the fundamental structure of and confidence in their democratic institutions.

The response from the Justice Department and U.S. law-enforcement officials has been narrow in scope; thus far, it's amounted to imposing sanctions on four known Russian agents for their alleged election-tampering efforts, and charging an employee of a Russian troll factory known as the "Internet Research Agency" with "criminal conspiracy to defraud the United States" (related to election influence). These cases notwithstanding, Putin is clearly winning Russia's hybrid war against the U.S. because Americans don't understand how they are being manipulated.

One of the main difficulties in countering malign Russian influence stems from divergent understandings of hybrid warfare. Russia considers hybrid warfare a form of conflict which includes strategic uses of economic, diplomatic, and influence operations, along with the use of military forces and espionage. By contrast, the U.S thinks of hybrid warfare as actions or tactics used before a conventional war. While the U.S. thinks it is managing pre-conflict aggression, Russia already considers itself in the midst of a strategic battle disguised as competitive aggression.

Since the 2016 elections, America's intelligence agencies have repeatedly warned about the threats to American elections posed by foreign states such as Russia. A 2017 Intelligence Community Assessment highlighted the efforts of foreign states who try to "shift U.S. policies, increase discord … and undermine the American people's confidence in the democratic process." In 2018, NBC News reported that U.S. intelligence had substantial evidence that Russian-backed operatives successfully targeted voter-registration systems in all 50 states prior to the 2016 election. More recently, Bill Evanina, who directs the National Counterintelligence and Security Center, revealed that Russia used various methods to "denigrate former Vice President Biden." The FBI and CISA also warned of foreign disinformation prior to recent elections, and U.S. intelligence agencies pointed to Russia, China, and Iran as the primary culprits in these malicious efforts.

Washington needs to be clear-eyed about the Kremlin's hybrid warfare operations, and must begin to anticipate Putin's intentions and identify ways to defend U.S. vulnerabilities. Additionally, the U.S. needs to counter Russian cyberattacks and dissemination of fake news globally. The U.S. should confront Russia with evidence of their malign behavior, and significantly increase information-sharing with friends and allies. This includes working closely with the EU's Special Committee on Foreign Interference and the European External Action Service, and assisting with the establishment a new specialized and coordinated agency for countering Russian disinformation. Former Defense secretary Mark Esper correctly noted that winning cyberspace requires an offensive strategy: The U.S. should not shy away from employing its offensive cyber capabilities against Russia. Cost-benefit analyses seem to indicate that the Kremlin recoils—or is routed—when Washington pushes back. The U.S.'s covert cyberattack against Russia's Internet Research Agency in 2018 during U.S. midterm elections is a perfect case in point.

The most significant step Washington can take, however, is to raise the level of international awareness concerning Russia's relentless use of disinformation to manipulate open societies. Putin's nefarious actions thrive on silence, and the current, muted international discourse on the matter represents a victory for the Kremlin. If Russia considers such meddling an act of "hybrid war" on its own terms, the U.S. would do well to address these efforts with commensurate vigor by calling out Russian disinformation publicly and taking retaliatory actions whenever possible.

Chapter 4

Has Recent Political Turmoil Undermined the US Position as the World's Leading Democracy?

Overview: Democratic Legitimacy Stems from Procedural and Institutional Integrity

Daniel I. Weiner and Tim Lau

Daniel I. Weiner is deputy director of the Election Reform Program at the Brennan Center for Justice. Tim Lau is a staff writer for the Communications and Strategy Team at the Brennan Center for Justice.

Since he was declared the winner of the 2020 election on Saturday, President-Elect Joe Biden and his team have started an informal transition planning process, which so far has included naming key staff members, outlining a policy agenda, and forming a Covid-19 advisory board. President Donald Trump, however, has refused to concede and attempted to cast doubt on the validity of the election, claiming without evidence that there was widespread voter fraud and other irregularities. His campaign has filed numerous meritless lawsuits to challenge the election results.

Meanwhile, many Republican leaders in Congress and in the administration have yet to acknowledge the outcome of the election. In remarks on Tuesday, Secretary of State Mike Pompeo went as far to suggest that "there will be a smooth transition to a second Trump administration." (He later claimed to be joking.) And Emily W. Murphy, the Trump-appointed head of the General Services Administration, has refused to formally recognize Biden as the election winner, delaying the start of the official presidential transition process.

To place these developments into context, the Brennan Center's Daniel I. Weiner spoke with Tim Lau and explained the significance of a peaceful transfer of power, the consequences of inadequate presidential transitions, and the potential for reform.

This interview has been edited for clarity and length.

"Why the Presidential Transition Process Matters," by Daniel I. Weiner and Tim Lau, Brennan Center for Justice at NYU Law, November 13, 2020. Reprinted by permission.

What is the significance of a peaceful transfer of power in a democracy like the United States?

A peaceful transfer of power—particularly from one political party to another—is, in my mind, the ultimate expression of the rule of law and of a society governed by the law, not by individual rulers. Say other things that you want about him, but it was George Washington's great contribution to the American political tradition when he voluntarily gave up the presidency. It established an unbroken tradition of presidents yielding power, including to their bitter political opponents. Even on the cusp of the Civil War, for example, James Buchanan never suggested that Abraham Lincoln wasn't entitled to become president after he won the election. That's what's so unprecedented with the current transition process, right? There is no legal path for Donald Trump to remain president. None. The spectacle of an incumbent president behaving this way is something we haven't seen before and is deeply corrosive to our democracy.

Who are the key players and institutions in the presidential transition, and why is it important that it's a nonpartisan process?

The presidential transition process exists both on a symbolic level and on a practical level. On the symbolic level, it has tremendous significance. The ritual of one president preparing to cede power to another signifies that we are a law-abiding society in which the will of the voters governs.

But there is also a practical level. The federal government of the United States is one of the largest organizations in the world, and the process of transferring control from one group of political actors to another is incredibly complex. There are thousands of real-time decisions that will have to be made from the moment the next president takes office. There are organizational competencies that have to be developed. So, we've developed this long-standing tradition where as soon as the result of the election becomes apparent, the incumbent administration—if the administration is changing—undertakes to help the incoming administration take up the reins.

I think what the rest of the world sees is the symbolic significance, and that's very important for America's credibility in the world and also for the confidence the American people have in their government (which is why Pompeo's joking is absolutely inexcusable). But in addition, the next president has to be ready to govern on day one. And if there isn't an adequate transition, that puts national security at risk, that puts American lives at risk—particularly given that the next president is going to have to wrestle with a global pandemic. And it just generally is terrible for government operations. As President George W. Bush's first chief of staff recently noted, the 9/11 Commission found that the truncated transition for the Bush administration from the Clinton administration was a contributing factor to our vulnerability to the terrorist attacks. We're playing with fire when we have the same thing happening here.

What elements of the presidential transition process, if any, are actually enshrined in the Constitution or in federal law?

As with so many core aspects of our government, the Constitution says almost nothing about presidential transitions, other than that the next president is going to take office on January 20.

The main federal statute, the Presidential Transition Act, was originally passed in 1963. It sets forth certain processes and requirements that govern both before and—if a new president is coming to power—after the election. The overall process is managed by the General Services Administration (GSA). For present purposes, the most important provision is the one that appears to leave it to the GSA administrator to "ascertain" whether a new president and vice president have been elected, which is the key to unlocking resources and access to federal agencies, including the all-important national security briefings. Since the administrator was appointed by and serves at the pleasure of the incumbent president, there is an obvious conflict of interest.

Again, though, until now no GSA administrator has ever tried to delay a transition in the wake of an election whose result was clear.

That's basically it. There's nothing that says the incumbent president must invite their successor to the White House or personally cooperate with them in any way. It's all just tradition—but again, tradition that no outgoing administration has ever flouted to the extent we are seeing now.

Let's discuss the current situation. Almost two weeks after the election, the president has not yet acknowledged the outcome. Neither have key senior officials like the vice president or the secretary of state. What kind of signal does that send to Americans and to the world?
Again, I really want to emphasize that these tactics aren't going to be successful. They are not going to keep Joe Biden from becoming the next president. According to the Department of Homeland Security's Cybersecurity and Infrastructure Security Agency—which is part of the Trump administration—this election "was the most secure in American history." The result is crystal clear.

But I think they are enormously corrosive to the foundation of our society. The damage to our standing in the world and to the confidence Americans can have in their government could be substantial.

In this regard, I really do want to focus on Secretary Pompeo. Recall that he already has violated a long-standing tradition of secretaries of state staying out of politics by, for instance, speaking at the Republican convention. His statement about a Trump second term—regardless of its intent—really does put him on par with, say, the foreign minister of Belarus (a country whose leader Pompeo himself has criticized for trying to cling to power by antidemocratic means). He's behaving like a regime thug, and that has done tremendous damage to the office of the secretary of state. It won't change the result, but it's still shameful.

I'd be remiss if I didn't also mention Attorney General Barr. He made some outrageous statements prior to the election that seemed to indicate a willingness to interfere with voting (which would have been illegal). On Monday he issued a memo authorizing Department of Justice (DOJ) prosecutors to investigate unsubstantiated claims of voter fraud before the results of the election are certified, which is a radical break from precedent.

This is almost certainly just posturing, as Brennan Center Vice President for Democracy Wendy Weiser recently explained. Without any evidence of widespread misconduct (which does not exist), there isn't much DOJ can do. But the fact remains that Barr has presided over a level of politicization at DOJ that we simply haven't seen in the modern era. It makes the Bush-era U.S. attorney firing scandal, which brought down a sitting attorney general and ruined his reputation, look positively tame.

What's happening with the transition didn't happen in a vacuum. We've seen a consistent effort to undermine the legitimacy of our elections.

In some ways, this is the culmination of something that's been going on for the better part of a year, which is a sustained effort to cast doubt on the legitimacy of our elections, really as a tactic for voter suppression and ultimately to try to make certain people's votes not count as much as other people's votes. And you see it's inevitably the votes coming from predominantly Black and brown communities, urban communities, that are somehow "suspect." That's been happening since long before the election. It happened with the president's threats to deploy troops to the polls (validated by Barr) and to encourage vigilantes to go to the polls to "watch" election workers and voters. He's tried to sow distrust in our system.

I think that there's a really big difference between wanting our democracy to work, but acknowledging very serious problems, and just a wholesale effort to undermine people's basic faith in the democratic process. The reality is that this election was an enormous logistical achievement. It actually ran very smoothly, all things considered. And that's due in large part to the tireless work of election officials, both Republican and Democratic. There's no basis in reality to cast serious doubt on the outcome. But Trump's team has been telegraphing that they would do exactly that for months if they lost, and now we are seeing it.

At the end of the day, though, the result just wasn't that close. Biden is currently ahead in Pennsylvania by almost 60,000 votes (and of course his national lead is more than 5 million). At this point, as the very conservative editorial board of the very conservative *Las Vegas Review Journal* recently pointed out, Trump is doing his own supporters a disservice by refusing to accept the inevitable.

What can be done to help ensure an accountable, transparent, and smooth transition process in the future?

You might start by placing more of a clear-cut obligation on incumbent administrations to provide information and otherwise cooperate with incoming administrations by a certain date, instead of vague statutory language that appears to leave it up to this one agency official—though I should note that the Biden transition team has said it is considering litigation, and they probably have pretty decent arguments that the statue, as it exists, doesn't give the administrator of the GSA carte blanche to just ignore the result of an election. But clearer baseline rules would help.

Congress could theoretically say: Look, within two or three days of the election, every candidate who plausibly could become president gets access to the information and the facilities necessary to accomplish a transition. Again, none of these problems are completely new, right? During Bush v. Gore, the Clinton administration just decided to not give either the George W. Bush team or the Al Gore team access. And they waited until the final resolution of that dispute. But again, that led to a truncated transition that may have negatively impacted our national security.

Beyond the narrow issue of presidential transitions, what is transpiring during the lame-duck period is just further proof that we need to codify some of the unwritten rules that the Trump administration has discarded, along the lines recommended by the Brennan Center's bipartisan task force. We need limits on White House interference with law enforcement, stronger implementation of ethics rules, better personnel practices, and much more. And of course we also need to repair many of the very real problems with our democracy that have helped to undermine confidence, which we can do by passing reforms like those in the landmark For the People Act, also known as H.R. 1. These have got to be priorities for the next president and Congress, and I think they will be. We have a lot of work to do.

Why the Crisis in American Politics Is Also a National Security Problem

Jon Bateman

Jon Bateman is a former official in the US Department of Defense and a fellow in the Cyber Policy Initiative of the Technology and International Affairs Program at the Carnegie Endowment for International Peace.

Last week's insurrection at the U.S. Capitol was the greatest national security crisis our country has faced in many decades. This may surprise Americans who have long been taught that "national security" means combating foreign threats and projecting U.S. influence abroad. No foreign power has attacked, and relatively few Americans died. Yet the American nation itself—its democratic core—was left destabilized and profoundly insecure. It should now be obvious that domestic dysfunction, not foreign hostility, is the real existential danger. This fact requires a wholesale rethinking of U.S. military, intelligence, and diplomatic priorities. National security experts must finally reconsider what "the nation" really is and what "securing" it really means.

Since 1945, U.S. national security strategy has undergone several distinct shifts: from the Cold War to the unipolar moment; from the war on terror to "great power competition." I had a front row seat to the most recent shift as a former special assistant to the chairman of the Joint Chiefs of Staff, General Joseph Dunford. Yet despite their differences, all these strategies reflected the same basic bargain between U.S. citizens and their government. Americans agreed to spend extraordinary amounts of money, human capital, and political attention on managing the world beyond their borders. In return, they hoped to expand and preserve their own prosperity and freedom.

"National Security in an Age of Insurrection," by Jon Bateman, Carnegie Endowment for International Peace, January 14, 2021. Reprinted by permission.

This bargain has often paid off. Western victory over the Soviet Union eliminated a major threat to liberal democracy. And Pax Americana helped to underwrite periods of broad-based U.S. economic growth. But in the last twenty years, something went awry. The conflicts after September 11 cost dearly in blood and treasure, yet U.S. adversaries—Islamic extremists and states like China, Russia, North Korea, and Iran—now loom larger than before. Even more troubling, America's own conditions have steadily deteriorated.

Politically, our system of government has reached a crisis point. Polarization, disinformation, and cynicism run rampant. More Americans are losing faith in government or the democratic process itself. This is partly understandable: politics have indeed become less responsive, with a broken Congress largely ignoring problems like opioid deaths and student debt for years on end.

Economically, the American dream has lost much of its luster. Rising costs of middle-class necessities like housing and healthcare outstrip wage growth, while social mobility has broadly declined. And people of color continue to fall behind, even as demographic and cultural changes fuel White grievance. These many problems feed into and fuse with one another, leading more and more Americans to reject the system as a whole.

It was these long-simmering, home-grown grievances—not China or the self-proclaimed Islamic State—that brought our country to the brink last week. A fracturing American system inspired an anti-system movement. With President Donald Trump as its avatar, this movement had managed to seize the reins of government, erode democracy from within, and violently resist the outcome of a free and fair election. Trump himself may fade from the scene, but our underlying sicknesses will remain. If we fail to address them, then Americans may well lose the very nation we hope to secure.

What, then, should the national security profession do about our fraying domestic order? Perhaps not much. The main culprits are political and economic leaders, after all—not soldiers, intelligence officers, or diplomats. But the latter group isn't altogether blameless. National security agencies suffer from the sins of gluttony (in devouring scarce resources) and pride (in making costly blunders). To help their country repair itself, these institutions need a little less swagger and a bit more candid reflection on the larger American project.

To begin with, we must acknowledge that many national security challenges are simply not as pressing as our dire need for domestic renewal. China will spend decades pursuing global parity with the United States, yet U.S. democracy could plausibly collapse in one or two election cycles. National security institutions and their supporters have so far failed to make this comparison. Each year, congressional appropriators label much-needed infrastructure investments and social services as mere "non-defense" spending, which must compete dollar for dollar with military programs.

In other cases, national security policies have directly contributed to domestic dysfunction. The Iraq War, for example, laid the groundwork for a more toxic, polarized, and anti-intellectual political climate. The war's stink of failure helped to discredit the entire U.S. political class, which Trump skillfully exploited in his 2016 presidential campaign.

I'm not alone in calling to realign U.S. national security strategy with America's needs at home. A growing number of figures on both the left and the right are proposing this. Trump's America First doctrine, while disastrous, at least reflected an instinctual awareness of the problem. Joe Biden's incoming administration, for its part, has promised a "foreign policy for the middle class" and intends to better integrate national security with domestic policy.

This is laudable, but it won't be easy to accomplish. Entrenched bureaucratic systems, professional cultures, and political realities make it hard for any president to overhaul the national security enterprise (as Trump himself often found). Biden will face pushback from career professionals and political constituencies who adhere to traditional views of national security. To overcome these headwinds, he will need to deliver two firm messages to his administration and the public.

First, national security institutions must better understand our most serious domestic challenges and learn to place them at the center of their work. In particular, they must tackle our crisis of democracy and the underlying economic, racial, and cultural grievances that fuel it.

In some policy areas, there is a clear path forward. The Department of Justice must prosecute all violent insurrectionists, and the FBI should step up investigations of white nationalists and other violent groups. Efforts to combat Russian and other foreign influence operations should be redoubled. And the U.S. government should harness its many experts on global democracy promotion, de-radicalization, and economic development— redeploying a portion of them to the home front.

Other issues will require more debate. It is clear, for example, that U.S. policy toward China should prioritize an economic relationship that brings hope to desperate American communities—even as we press Beijing on human rights, military matters, and other points of tension. But experts disagree about how exactly to do this. The important thing for now is to set the presidential objective, so that policy debates are about means rather than ends.

Importantly, a formal requirement to consider domestic impacts may dissuade national security officials from recommending counterproductive actions. Consider Trump's crackdown on the Chinese app TikTok, which had substantial support in the national security community. Trump's actions, whatever their benefits, nevertheless smacked of crony capitalism and risked anti-competitive effects—potentially worsening two specific challenges the United States faces at home. It is doubtful that Trump weighed these pros and cons; Biden will need to do so.

Refocusing national security agencies on domestic problems is the first step. But their tools can only do so much to address political and economic challenges. That is why Biden will need to deliver a second, more difficult message. He must ask national security institutions to yield center stage—ceding some money, talent, and attention to those who can directly help mend our nation.

Former defense secretary Jim Mattis once told Congress, "If you don't fund the State Department fully, then I need to buy more ammunition ultimately." His point was that national security as a whole suffers when just one element predominates; we must take a broader approach that accounts for interlinkages. Mattis was right, but he didn't go far enough. We need diplomats and soldiers, yes—but our greatest needs today are civics teachers, election officials, public broadcasters, and social workers. National security leaders should loudly promote government investments in these areas, even at some cost to their own budgets.

This shift will involve people as well as money. America's premier national security organizations—for example, the CIA and the military service academies—leverage their prestige to attract highly promising young people. We need similar talent pipelines for community organizers, civil rights lawyers, and many others who can help bind the nation's internal wounds. National security leaders should actively encourage ambitious young people to enter these fields, accepting that some talent would be diverted from their own organizations.

Finally, the U.S. government must better allocate its attention. National security agencies have a unique hold on the president's time and mental bandwidth, embodied in rituals like the President's Daily Brief. Recent presidents have helpfully broadened the brief to cover more "economic intelligence." But the overall balance of power in the White House remains quite uneven: the National Security Council is many times larger than the National Economic Council and the Domestic Policy Council combined. Biden will need new structures to ensure that key domestic issues—like the evolving media landscape, or the economic mobility of Black Americans—remain on the front burner amid inevitable foreign flare-ups.

These changes would come at a cost. A realignment toward domestic matters will inevitably take something away from the rest of U.S. foreign policy. Many national security experts want even more U.S. investment in its traditional global priorities, and they have legitimate concerns. The U.S. military really is falling behind its competitors. Islamic extremism really has metastasized. A rising China really will bully other nations, hollow out their industries, and export authoritarianism. Any reshuffling of priorities must still find some balance between the foreign and domestic. It will be crucial to consult with allies along the way.

But the status quo presents far greater risks. Last week's coup attempt helps put everything into perspective. While international threats are growing, domestic crises have already spiraled out of control. If we look the other way as the U.S. Constitution comes apart, then "national security" becomes all but meaningless.

Let's hope that future presidents can deftly manage China, contain Iran's nuclear program, and prevent major cyber attacks. But suppose the price of these successes is failure to reverse our democracy's downward slide. What then would we be left with as Americans? After last week's events, the question can no longer be avoided. If nothing changes, then the United States will eventually be unable to survive in its current form. Such an outcome, for any country, is the ultimate national security failure.

American Democracy Is Facing a Long-Term Crisis

Sandra Feder

Sandra Feder is a writer, editor, and public relations communications officer at Stanford University. Interviewee Terry Moe is the William Bennett Munro Professor of Political Science, and William Howell is the Sydney Stein Professor of American Politics, both at the University of Chicago.

The United States is facing a historic crisis that fundamentally threatens our democratic system of government, according to Stanford political scientist Terry Moe.

"The nation has entered a treacherous new era in its history, one that threatens the system of self-government that for more than two hundred years has defined who we are as a country and as a people," write Moe, the William Bennett Munro Professor in Political Science in the School of Humanities and Sciences, and William Howell, the Sydney Stein Professor in American Politics at the University of Chicago, in a new book, *Presidents, Populism, and the Crisis of Democracy* (University of Chicago Press).

In the book the pair argues that while critics see Donald Trump as the most visible threat to our system of self-government, his presidency is really a symptom of long brewing forces. These forces include globalization, automation and immigration, which have created economic disruptions and cultural anxieties for millions of Americans.

"Our government has done a very ineffective job of dealing with these problems and the result has been a rising surge of populist anger," Moe said in an interview.

"Stanford Scholar Says Major Reforms Are Needed to Save Our Democracy," by Sandra Feder, Stanford University, August 10, 2020. Courtesy Stanford News Service. Reprinted by permission.

Saving our democracy, the scholars write, will require major changes that go beyond November's election. The real challenge, they contend, is to enact programs and institutional reforms that can provide us with a genuinely effective government—one that is capable of dealing with the problems of modernity and defusing the populist threat. Until that challenge is met, they say, reformers cannot rest.

"The fact is, no matter which party holds the presidency, these are not normal times," the authors write. "And a sense of normalcy, should it take hold with the election of a new president, stands to be little more than an exercise in denial, offering temporary relief from the recent populist turmoil but leaving the causes of that turmoil unaddressed and the potential for continued democratic backsliding firmly in place."

Decades of Discontent

The new book contends that the current crisis did not happen overnight but is the result, in part, of the globalization that began in the late 1970s and 1980s, taking jobs out of many U.S. communities and leaving millions of workers disaffected and angry.

Another blow to U.S. workers was a rise in automation, making many jobs obsolete. The ineffectual response of the government to the plight of these workers, Moe said, eventually led many to embrace President Donald Trump's populist message in 2016.

"We can't stop globalization or automation," he said, "but we need to compensate those most affected by providing them with subsidies, education, job training and more, through programs that are truly effective." The workers most affected were less-educated working-class whites, often in rural communities, and particularly men.

These Americans also felt an acute cultural anxiety, the authors contend, including an impending loss of privilege and culture as the U.S. became more diverse, urban, cosmopolitan and secular.

Now, COVID-19 is exacerbating existing economic insecurities. "But it also provides an opportunity for government to step in and provide action," said Moe.

Balancing Presidential Power

The U.S. president has historically been a champion of effective government, which is why the authors focus their solutions to the current crisis on changes to the presidency.

"Presidents are primarily motivated by their legacies, so they want to design policies that work to solve social problems," Moe said. "We need to take advantage of the great promise of the presidency to promote effective government by giving presidents more power in respect to Congress." The scholars consider President Trump, and what they see as his disdain for many aspects of U.S. government, as a historical outlier. The scholars argue that another reason to focus on the presidency is that Congress is a more parochial institution, comprising 535 people who might be more concerned about what's best for their districts and states rather than what's best for the nation as a whole.

In the book, the scholars offer one significant reform designed to enhance presidential authority: allowing a president to submit legislation to Congress that would be fast-tracked and would have to be voted up or down without changes. Both houses of Congress would still need to pass the legislation and the courts could still weigh in on legal issues. Under this proposal, Congress also could still draft its own legislation, which the president could choose to veto or sign.

The goal of this process would allow the one political actor who might best have the nation's overall interests at heart—the president—to present a complete piece of legislation with potentially far-reaching solutions.

Of course, the downside of this approach, according to the authors, is that we have good reason to fear presidential power. "We don't want to give the president the power to destroy our democracy," Moe said. "So we also have a number of reforms in the book designed to constrain presidential power."

In order to maintain a balance and curb the presidential power that the authors believe hinders effective government, they propose:

- Making the Department of Justice and intelligence agencies independent of presidential control. One way to accomplish this would be to have them run by bipartisan multi-member boards, in the same way that the Federal Communications Commission and the Securities and Exchange Commission are.
- Dramatically restricting presidential appointments and relying more on career civil servants.
- Eliminating the president's pardon power, which would require a constitutional amendment.
- Increasing anti-corruption rules and regulations to better avoid conflicts of interest on the part of the president.

Lessons from Prior Eras

According to the authors, there are lessons for modern times that can be learned from both the Progressive Era of U.S. politics under President Theodore Roosevelt and the New Deal under President Franklin Roosevelt.

"The Progressives gave us a modern government," Moe said. "They replaced the spoils system with civil service." Then, when the Great Depression hit, Franklin Roosevelt's New Deal programs were designed to deal with the deep economic problems of the country by putting people back to work.

"That's the kind of thing this country needs now," Moe said. "We need something big and transformative. If we want to save our democracy, we must focus on building a truly effective government that is capable of dealing with the basic problems of the modern world. If that can't be done, populist anger will continue to surge."

Trump May Have Challenged Norms, But the Institutions That Support American Democracy Are Secure

Elaine Kamarck

Elaine Kamarck is director of the Center for Effective Public Management and a senior fellow in the Governance Studies Program at the Brookings Institution. She is also a lecturer in public policy at Harvard University's Kennedy School of Government.

Did Trump permanently damage American democracy? This question has spawned a veritable cottage industry of hand wringing over the state of American democracy—understandably so. Never before have we had a president who schemed to overturn legitimate election results, who attacked the press and the civil servants who worked for him, who admired dictators, who blatantly profited from his public office and who repeatedly lied to the public for his own selfish purposes. But while Trump's four years of rhetoric have been a shock to democratic norms, did they inflict permanent damage on our democracy? My answer is a qualified no. The guardrails of democracy held. The institutions designed to check autocracy are intact.

Successful democratic systems are not designed for governments composed of ethical men and women who are only interested in the public good. If leaders were always virtuous there would be no need for checks and balances. The Founding Fathers understood this. They designed a system to protect minority points of view and to protect us from leaders inclined to lie, cheat and steal. Fortunately, we haven't had many of those in our 200-plus years of history, which is why the Trump presidency sent such shock waves through a large part of the body politic.

"Did Trump Damage American Democracy?" by Elaine Kamarck, The Brookings Institution, July 9, 2021. Reprinted by permission.

Those who bemoan Trump's effect on democracy complain that he did not adhere to the established norms of the presidency. That is correct; he is, at heart, a dictator. But let's start by distinguishing between norms and institutions. Norms are different from laws; they are not enforceable and they evolve. In contrast, democratic institutions are based in law and entail real consequences. Changes in norms can in fact lead to changes in law and in democratic institutions—this has happened in many of the countries in eastern Europe and Latin America that have slipped into pseudo-democracy or autocracy.[1] But in spite of Donald Trump's best efforts it has not happened here. At least not yet.

To get a sense of why I argue that the guardrails of democracy have held, let's look at the five major institutions that protect us from rule by an aspiring dictator: Congress, the courts, the federal system, the press and the civil service. Not a single one of them has lost legal power during Trump's turbulent presidency. Refusing to use power is not the same as losing the power.

Did Trump Weaken the Powers of Congress? No.

Nancy Pelosi had no trouble confronting Trump, as is evident to anyone who has seen the iconic photo of her standing up in the Cabinet room and pointing at Donald Trump as she lectured him. Democrats brought impeachment charges against Trump not once but twice. Although speculation was rampant, in the end then-Majority Leader Mitch McConnell (R-KY) did not block either trial. Trump did not try to disband Congress, nor did he try to pass laws that weakened its most important power, the power of the purse. In fact, at no point during the Trump years did Trump attempt to formally weaken congressional power.

Those who argue that Trump weakened democracy often don't distinguish policy from democratic process. While Mitch MConnell and allies have been called Trump's lapdogs, on domestic policy they have acted like almost any Republican majority would act, siding with business on issues like cutting taxes, regulations and liability protections. And on foreign policy McConnell did not stop nor punish Republican senators who tried to constrain Trump when they thought he was wrong.[2]

Has Trump Damaged Our System of Shared Power Between the Federal Government and the States? No.

The Constitution distributes power between the federal government and the state government, codified in the 10th Amendment to the Constitution: "The powers not delegated to the United States by the Constitution, nor prohibited by it to the States, are reserved to the States respectively, or to the people." It took Trump a long time to understand this but states have repeatedly exercised their power against Trump, especially in two areas; COVID-19 and voting.

In the spring of 2020 Trump, anxious to get past COVID in time for his re-election campaign, was pushing hard for states to open up early. Democratic governors ignored Trump's demands to open up. In some states, Republican governors tried acting like mini-Trumps, in others they gave him lip service but did not open up completely, and in Ohio Republican Governor Mike DeWine politely disagreed and kept the state closed. Trump, seeing that the governors were not scared of him, then threatened to withold medical equipment based on states' decisions about opening up. He came up against the 10th Amendment, which prevents the president from conditioning federal aid on the basis of governors acquiescing to a president's demands. Trump couldn't use the cudgel he thought he had.

The guardrails between the federal government and the states also held when it came to Trump's campaign to win the election.

In Georgia the courageous Republican Secretary of Brad Raffensperger, a stalwart Republican and Trump supporter, certified election results in spite of personal calls and threats from the president. In Michigan, Republican Senate Majority Leader

Mike Shirkey and Republican House Speaker Lee Chatfield did not give in to Trump's attempts to get them to diverge from the process of choosing electors.

So did Trump inflict lasting damage to our Federalist system? Are governors weaker than they were pre-Trump? If anything citizens now understand that in a crisis, governors are the ones who control things that are important to them like shutdown orders and vaccine distribution. Trump's campaign to convince governors to take actions to suppress the vote remains a huge problem for democracy but it is succeeding not because Trump had dictatorial powers over the states but because he has like-minded allies in many state houses and state legislatures.

Has Trump Weakened the Judiciary? No.

One of the hallmarks of dictators is that they weaken the judiciary so that courts rubber-stamp their every whim. But to Trump's dismay he discovered that appointing conservative judges is not the same as controlling judges the way someone like Vladimir Putin does. Trump's first controversial act as president—the famous Muslim ban—was repeatedly struck down by the courts until the administration drafted a version that could pass legal muster.

When it came to trying to overturn the results of the 2020 election, Trump-appointed judges often made decisions that thwarted Trump's attempts at denying the results. Take, for instance, the following from Judge Stephanos Bibas, a Trump appointee on the 3rd Circuit, writing for the three-judge panel in Pennsylvania:

> Free, fair elections are the lifeblood of our democracy. Charges of unfairness are serious. But calling an election unfair does not make it so. Charges require specific allegations and then proof. We have neither here.

In fact, after the election Trump's team brought 62 lawsuits and won one. The others he either dropped or he lost and many of those decisions were made by Republican judges. Perhaps his biggest disappointment had to be the Supreme Court's decision to not hear election challenges from states Trump believed he had won.

Did Trump Weaken the Press? No.

Trump spent four years using the bully pulpit of the presidency to mock the press, calling them names and "the enemy of the people" and referring to outlets he doesn't like as "failing." He revoked the press credentials from reporters he didn't like. (Although the courts restored them.) Reporters have not been afraid to call out his lies. With Trump out of office for months now, no major news outlets have gone broke. None are afraid to criticize Trump or his supporters.

The free press is still free and fairly healthy. Its financial and structural problems have to do with their adaptation to the internet age, all of which predated Trump.

Some argue that Trump increased distrust in the media but as a Gallup poll indicates, the lack of trust in the media fell in around 2008 has been largely constant since then.

Was Trump Able to Exert Control Over the Civil Service? No.

The United States government is based on the rule of law, not the rule of men. Nowhere is that more evident than in the behavior of the career civil service or the permanent government. In dictatorships there is no such thing as a "career" civil service—only loyalists who act on dictates from the man, not the law. Early on, Trump found out that he could not prevent the appointment of a Special Counsel to investigate his relations with Russia. Where the law allowed for discretion and where career government officials could legally implement a presidential order—as in the disastrous separation of children at the border—the career civil servants acted as Trump wished. But where the law was clear Trump could not force his will on the bureaucracy.

Take, for instance, Trump's desire to announce a successful vaccine for the coronavirus before Election Day. When the Food and Drug Administration wrote guidelines that would govern when a pharmaceutical company could get emergency-use authorization to begin distributing vaccines, the Trump administration tried to block them because it would mean release of the vaccines after the election. The attempt to politicize a scientific process was not well received by FDA employees and career scientists, who in defiance of the White House went ahead and published the vaccine guidelines, which the Trump administration then "approved" after the fact.

Frustrated by the many "veto points" in the system, Trump took to issuing executive actions, many of which were focused on the environment. But once again he did not see the limits of his powers. According to a Brookings study:

> Many of the Trump administration's measures, environmental or otherwise, have failed to stand up in court, with the administration losing 83 percent of litigations.

While Trump has been able to weaken environmental regulations, the courts and the system itself proved to be guardrails. As of the last year of his administration less than half of his environmental regulatory actions (48 out of 84) were in effect. The others were either in process or have been repealed or withdrawn—often after the administration lost in court.

Conclusion

The fact that Trump did not tear down the major guardrails of democracy does not mean that all is well in the United States. He attracted the support of millions of voters in 2020 and, even more dangerous is the fact that much of the Republican Party still insists on refuting the results of that election and weakening non-partisan election administration in certain states where they hold legislative majorities. Norms have been broken and could yet result in majorities that overturn laws and weaken institutions. It's possible that had Trump been more experienced in government he could have been able to amass the powers he so wanted to have. The lesson is that democracy requires constant care and constant mobilization.

But all in all, my bet is that the Founding Fathers would be proud of the way the system they designed stood up to and thwarted King Trump. The guardrails held: Congress was not disbanded and its powers were not weakened, the states retained substantial power and authority over their own citizens, the courts displayed their independence and ability to stand up to the presidency, the press remained free and critical and the bureaucracy held to the rule of law, not the whim of man.

Notes

1. See William A. Galston, *Anti-Pluralism: The Populist Threat to Liberal Democracy.*

2. In July 2017 Congress passed a Russian sanctions bill that included in it a unique provision limiting Trump's ability to lift sanctions unilaterally. The bill was opposed by the White House but passed the House 419 to 3 and the Senate 98 to 2—meaning it was veto proof. The constraint on presidential action was a major step thwarting Trump's romance with Putin.

   Since then Republican senators have been openly critical of Trump on a variety of other foreign policy moves: many Republican senators condemned his praise of Putin at the 2018 Helsinki summit, some joined Democrats in opposing Trump actions in Yemen and 2/3 of House Republicans joined Democrats in condemning Trump's actions in Syria. Some Republicans joined Democrats in opposing Trump's declaration of an emergency at the southwest border. In 2020, Republicans joined Democrats in a bill to rename bases that had been named after Confederate leaders and Trump did not veto it.

How America Can Lead a Global Revitalization of Democracy

Kelly Magsamen, Max Bergmann, Michael Fuchs, and Trevor Sutton

Kelly Magsamen is an American foreign policy expert currently serving as chief of staff to the US Secretary of Defense in the Biden administration. Max Bergmann is a senior fellow at the Center for American Progress and a former official in the US Department of State. Michael Fuchs is a senior fellow at the Center for American Progress and a foreign policy adviser to former president Bill Clinton. Trevor Sutton is a national security and international policy expert and a senior fellow at the Center for American Progress.

[…]

Donald Trump is hardly the only skeptic of a democratic values-based foreign policy. A range of policymakers and scholars of foreign policy, including some progressives, have argued that the United States should de-prioritize the promotion of democratic values in its foreign policy. Some make the argument that the United States needs to take a more hardheaded and transactional approach to advance its security and economic interests. However, this report argues that not only are these false choices but that the United States should see democratic values as a U.S. comparative advantage—and not a weakness—in global competition. America's liberal democratic values have been key to building, enhancing, and sustaining America's geopolitical power. With the global backsliding of democracy and the rise of alternative authoritarian models, it is ever more urgent to rediscover the power of core American values to secure U.S. interests in the long term. A democratic values-based foreign policy is worth pursuing for three key reasons.

"Securing a Democratic World," by Kelly Magsamen, Max Bergmann, Michael Fuchs, and Trevor Sutton, Center for American Progress, September 5, 2018. Reprinted by permission.

First, it will advance long-term U.S. economic and security interests abroad and create a safer and more prosperous world. Compared with authoritarian regimes, democracies are less likely to go to war against each other, less likely to ally against the United States, less likely to sponsor terrorism, less likely to experience famine or produce refugees, and more likely to adopt market economies and form economic partnerships with other democracies.[35] Since liberal democracies tend to share values rooted in rule of law, fair competition, and transparency, they are natural partners in promoting the stable, prosperous, open, and peaceful international environment that the United States ought to cultivate through its foreign policy.

It is true that the process of democratization can be long and uneven and can sometimes produce destabilizing and aggressive state behavior. However, mature and established democracies are more stable, peaceful, and prosperous, and more full-fledged democracies mean more economic and security benefits for the United States.[36] Furthermore, the global system of democratic alliances, institutions, and norms the United States helped create and lead after World War II has improved material conditions and brought peace and prosperity to hundreds of millions of people across the world. Bolstering that democratic system and the democratic values that underpin it will ensure that future generations can also enjoy the fruits of democracy and a liberal world.

Second, this kind of foreign policy will help secure an American advantage in great power competition by advancing a compelling alternative and strengthening the global democratic bulwark. Although the challenge posed by illiberal regimes today has evolved since the Cold War, there are still lessons to be drawn from that era. One of the most significant factors in the collapse of the Soviet Union was the powerful example and contrast set by flourishing democratic societies in the United States and Europe. Today, one of America's greatest strategic assets is its global network of democratic allies and partners. The power of that democratic network, even underutilized as it is today, stands in stark contrast to what today's illiberal and authoritarian regimes can offer: namely, political order purchased at the cost of extreme corruption, xenophobia, oligarchy, and arbitrary use of state power. To succeed, any approach to countering the authoritarian playbook must present a compelling alternative. This means that the United States, alongside its democratic allies and partners, must demonstrate that liberal democracy represents the best path to deliver inclusive prosperity, rule of law, and a just and equal society to a country's citizens.

Third, it is the right thing to do. For more than a century, U.S. support for global democracy promotion has rested in part on the sincere conviction that all people deserve to have a say in how they are governed and enjoy the freedoms afforded people in liberal democracies. Although the United States has at many junctures acted in ways that undermined the expansion of democracy and democratic freedoms, that failure does not make democracy promotion any less worthy a goal for U.S. foreign policy. Put simply, there is intrinsic moral value in using the immense influence and capabilities of the United States to empower ordinary people across the globe.

The Way Forward: A Democracy-Rebalance Agenda for the Next Administration

To achieve these aims, the United States should implement a "democracy rebalance" designed to defend the existing liberal international order, motivate and empower global democracies to work together, and stem the rising tide of illiberalism. This effort would need to be more than a rhetorical shift. It would require Washington to undertake a strategic prioritization of effort to make protecting and advancing democracy a central pillar of the U.S. national security strategy. This strategic shift should be guided by the following principles:

- First, the incentives must be significant. The United States and its democratic allies must generate enough of a pull factor through economic, political, and security benefits to incentivize transitional democracies to continue along the democratic path and to help consolidate democratic gains in both new and established democracies.

- Second, there is strength in numbers. When providing incentives—and pushing back against illiberalism—the United States and its democratic partners need to lock arms to maximize effectiveness in an increasingly competitive global environment.
- Third, this must be a strategic priority that reorients and draws on all the tools of American statecraft. The focus of U.S. foreign policy often is pulled in various directions, but this democracy rebalance would require vigorous strategic prioritization.
- Fourth, democracy should not be spread through use of force. Military force should always be the last resort and only employed to address severe or acute security crises—not to advance a preferred political system. Resilient democratic governance is only possible through patient and sustained commitment to building effective democratic institutions. Military force will never be a substitute for this tried and tested approach.
- Fifth, the United States should seek to avoid acting unilaterally. Rather, it should practice humility and seek to work with and learn from countries that have pushed back successfully against the authoritarian playbook.
- Sixth, the most powerful force for global democracy will always be the aspirations of ordinary people. While it is natural for policymakers to focus on incentives and pressure points for foreign governments, the most durable and profound democratic change has historically come from grassroots, bottom-up movements. To that end, the United States and its partners should be prepared to

support and defend the rights of people around the world to mobilize nonviolently in support of greater civil and political freedoms.

How Should the United States Define Democracy?

This report considers the term "democracy" to encompass the consent of the governed and basic freedoms such as freedom of speech and assembly, a free press, equality before the law, free and fair elections, checks and balances, and protection of basic human rights as enshrined in the Universal Declaration of Human Rights, among other international agreements and conventions. But assessing which countries qualify as democratic for the purposes of U.S. foreign policy will inevitably require judgment calls. Fortunately, there are already several sets of criteria available for determining the strength of a country's democracy, such as the Polity IV Project index and the V-Dem Institute's Liberal Democracy Index.[37] Some of these criteria are already incorporated into how the Millennium Challenge Corporation (MCC), a U.S. foreign aid agency, determines which countries are eligible to receive its assistance. Other U.S. assistance programs may wish to do the same.

Policy Recommendations

Revitalizing global democracy is an immense and complex task that will take many years. But in the short term, the threat presented by opportunist authoritarian regimes urgently requires a rapid response. That is why America's democracy rebalance needs both an immediate defensive line of effort to protect democratic values at home and around the world from creeping authoritarianism and a sustained long-term effort to expand the global democratic community and address the drivers of democratic retrenchment.

Strengthen Democracy at Home

American foreign policy starts at home with the strength of our own democratic model. None of the initiatives proposed in this report is likely to succeed if the United States does not embrace its own democratic values and norms and lead by example. The next administration will need to simultaneously re-establish international credibility and strengthen the democratic compact with its own citizens. For the United States to compete effectively in the global battle of ideas, it must continue to perfect its own democracy and leverage its own comparative strengths: rule of law, strong institutions, the ability to self-correct as a nation, and the innovation and perseverance of the American people. While domestic policy is not the focus of this report, the authors felt it was essential to draw the connection between the health of American democracy and the strategic impact that the United States can drive globally in the context of rising competition.

Restore Democratic Values and Norms

The next administration will need to emphasize its adherence to democratic norms, including reaffirming and embracing the role of a free press, respecting the independence of the judiciary and law enforcement, valuing its civil servants, rejecting racial and religious antagonism, and separating the interests of the public from the private interests of those in power. A series of strong and clear measures in this direction in the early days of the next administration will be a necessary predicate to restoring American credibility abroad.

Build Trust in Science and Facts

With the assault on science and facts by the Trump administration and its allies—removing publicly available information on climate change from government agency websites, for instance, and certain conservative media outlets pushing baseless claims—it will be imperative for the U.S. government to ensure that policy decisions are driven by data and science and that information about policies are communicated objectively and clearly.[38]

Address Drivers of Declining Public Trust

The next administration will need to demonstrate that it can deliver for all Americans and restore the basic compact between the governed and the governing. That means mounting an effective response to entrenched economic inequality, structural racism, gun violence, poor health outcomes, the dominance of special interests, and persistent poverty and the challenges that accompany it, including rising drug addiction. Without confronting these scourges head-on, America cannot effectively advocate for and support liberal democracy abroad.[39]

Ensure a Free and Fair Democratic Process

For the United States to advance democracy abroad, it is essential that its democratic processes serve as a model, not as a cautionary tale. Currently, U.S. democratic processes are plagued by gerrymandering, a campaign finance system that strongly favors wealthy private interests, and weak transparency rules that distort democratic outcomes. The next administration, in conjunction with Congress, must seek to make meaningful headway against these counter-majoritarian practices.

Counter Authoritarianism and Vigorously Defend the Democratic Community of Nations

The United States and its democratic allies are on the front end of a long-term fight to defend their democratic processes as well as their free and open societies from foreign interference and political influence at the hand of authoritarian states. Democracies are not operating on a level playing field: Russia and China have a structural advantage of being closed societies where democratic ideas struggle to compete due to censorship, but neither Russia nor China shy away from engaging in efforts to exploit the open systems of the United States and other democratic countries.[40] For these reasons, it is essential that the United States design a more coherent, aggressive, and coordinated response to authoritarian encroachment.

To stem the authoritarian tide and defend democratic processes and institutions, democratic governments will also need the tools and knowledge to push back against the favorite tactics of illiberal regimes seeking to weaken and divide democratic societies. The United States should plan accordingly and lead a collaborative multilateral effort to counter the authoritarian playbook. This plan should involve several lines of effort, including:

- Insulating democratic processes from outside interference and closing vulnerabilities that authoritarian adversaries exploit, for example: outdated and vulnerable electoral infrastructure, porous campaign finance regimes, cybersecurity vulnerabilities in electoral bodies and political campaigns, and weak regulatory frameworks for addressing false or misleading information online[41]
- Encouraging digital media platforms, social networks, and data firms—the vast majority of which have lacked effective policies for identifying and deterring malign influence operations—to serve as a force for openness, not a tool to be abused by autocrats
- Addressing gaps in the international financial system and domestic laws that enable corruption, money laundering, and illegal campaign finance
- Identifying and sanctioning criminal actors that subvert democratic outcomes by advancing the interests of foreign powers in politics, media, and strategically important economic sectors
- Modernizing U.S. public diplomacy and increasing support to free and independent international broadcast media to better address and rebut the anti-democratic narratives offered by authoritarian regimes

These efforts will only succeed if executed in tandem with other democracies. Some of these lines of effort are likely to advance quickly, while others will take substantial time and investment.

Build Global Democratic Solidarity

Facing an illiberal challenge to the foundations of democratic society, the United States should endeavor to build a liberal bulwark. The first step in this project would be to catalyze deeper cooperation among democratic states. This will require a multipronged diplomatic effort that strengthens a variety of different multilateral and ad hoc networks of democratic states.

Network Security Alliances

From Europe to Asia and beyond, the United States has formal alliances with a wide range of democracies that constitute some of the world's most advanced and powerful defense capabilities. The United States should knit together these countries into a broader security architecture to enable better collaboration on regional and global security issues. An increase in security dialogues, technology sharing, and even exercises and interoperability amongst U.S. treaty allies could help bolster the power that democratic countries can project when confronted with global security challenges, from peacekeeping to deterrence to maritime security.

Transform the Community of Democracies into an Action-Oriented Summit of Democracies

The next administration should seek to transform the existing Community of Democracies (CD) into an annual Summit of Democracies that drives action on key challenges. Currently, the CD is an informal organization that gathers democracies to discuss challenges to democratic governance and to provide technical support to one another on building democratic institutions. Transforming the CD into a more effective institution would require two steps: First, reorient the organization to focus not only on shared threats to democratic societies—corruption, information warfare, and foreign interference in elections—but also shared strategic challenges, such as maritime security and interstate aggression; and second, convene the CD at the head-of-state level annually to endow it with the necessary political and bureaucratic buy-in and follow-through that it currently lacks. Like the idea of a "League of Democracies"[42] championed in the past by Sen. John McCain (R-AZ), this organization would be action-oriented—not as a replacement for existing international institutions but to provide an additional, exclusive venue through which leaders of new and transitioning democracies could build relationships with each other and their peers in established democracies. As President Barack Obama's nuclear security summits demonstrated, the constructive use of the bully pulpit of an American president can be a potent tool in marshaling complex international action.

Promote Informal Collaboration Among Democracies to Solve Key Global Challenges

The future of international cooperation on major global challenges is likely to be driven primarily by flexible, ad hoc arrangements of like-minded states. Many of these challenges would benefit from the specific cooperation of democracies, as well as regional organizations that make democracy a defining criteria of membership, such as the Organization of American States, the African Union, NATO, and the European Union. The United States should embrace this format of democratic cooperation and form new groupings, especially to act on challenges where democratic principles make a qualitative difference, such as corruption, development, humanitarian crises, and cybersecurity. Such arrangements can play a crucial role in demonstrating that democracies can act effectively and decisively to effect positive change and address pressing problems.

Upgrade the Tools of U.S. Statecraft to Privilege U.S. Policy Toward Democracies

The historic challenge of U.S. democracy promotion efforts is twofold: First, policies that advance democracy can be easily subordinated to near-term security and economic imperatives, and second, democracy promotion efforts are usually under-resourced and not well integrated into broader national security objectives. In a competitive world where the battle of ideas is becoming more intense and the value of the democratic model more contested, the next administration will need to recalibrate and upgrade the tools of U.S. democratic statecraft with the objective of privileging U.S. relationships with democracies and reversing the global democratic slide.

Elevate Democracy as a National Security Priority

Previous U.S. administrations have treated democracy promotion as a noble aspiration but not a key security interest and have accordingly subordinated it to a range of other foreign policy objectives such as counterterrorism, nonproliferation, and economic relations. Going forward, the United States must treat support for democracies as a strategic priority and seek to integrate it with other national security goals. This would translate into a shift from how the United States has traditionally conducted its foreign policy and deployed its powerful tools of statecraft to a new approach that confers special benefits on democracies. While the United States spends significant assistance on democracies—mostly through the MCC and specific economic and democracy assistance programs run by the U.S. Agency for International Development and the State Department—these efforts are diffuse and do not include coordinated whole-of-government efforts to combine economic assistance with security assistance, trade incentives, and other tools.

Launch a Democratic Strategic Advantage Initiative

The next U.S. administration should present a multiyear, multibillion-dollar proposal to Congress to create and fund a Democratic Strategic Advantage initiative—akin to past large-scale U.S. government efforts to fight AIDS worldwide—to help established democracies and emerging democratic states sustain progress and to give them a strategic advantage over authoritarian competitors. This initiative would authorize the U.S. government to amplify and better synchronize U.S. economic and security assistance and commercial investment packages. For example, in addition to increased economic assistance, the United States should coordinate its current tools for security cooperation— from arms sales to military training to technology transfer—to give democracies a strategic edge over authoritarian adversaries.

Increase Funding for Bipartisan Democracy Organizations
To amplify impact, the United States should ensure that all tools of democracy promotion abroad are running at full speed and able to operate with maximum effectiveness. Congress should accordingly expand funding for the National Endowment for Democracy, the National Democratic Institute, and the International Republican Institute, all of which invest in and work to strengthen democracy worldwide.

Support and Defend Democratic Voices

Most of the successful democratic transitions of the past two decades—such as those in Serbia (2000), Georgia (2003), Nepal (2006), Tunisia (2011), and Ukraine (2014)—had their origins in grassroots movements advocating for peaceful democratic change. Nonviolent resistance can be a powerful tool in pushing back against democratic backsliding, as recent anti-government protests in Armenia and Slovakia illustrate.[43] Yet the United States and its democratic partners do not yet have a strategy for engaging, supporting, and defending the rising number of nonviolent pro-democracy movements around the world, in part because of their diffuse, grassroots nature and in part out of concern that external assistance could undermine the legitimacy of such movements. These are valid concerns, but they should not stand in the way of a deliberate and thoughtful approach to peaceful protest. At a minimum, the United States should seek to work with international partners to strengthen international norms regarding the rights of citizens to mobilize peacefully for greater political and civil rights and engage in nonviolent protest against their respective governments.

A key component of this strategy must include significantly ramping up support for civil society in U.S. government programs and policies. In addition to the measure mentioned above, the United States must also make clear that support for nonviolent democracy movements is not about regime change or picking political winners; it is about supporting the universal rights of people to engage in peaceful political expression. Lastly, the United States should seek to deter and punish states that violently crack down on their own people. The United States should make clear that violent repression will trigger strong U.S. economic sanctions and diplomatic isolation.

[...]

Conclusion

For more than 70 years, the United States' ability to do good in the world and secure its international interests has been inseparable from its commitment to democracy at home and abroad. Today, just as democracies around the world face new challenges from without and within, President Trump is chipping away day by day at America's standing as a force for good in the world.

The present age is not the first time that the United States has seen global democracy in retreat or presided over the decline of its own influence. History has proven more than once that the United States is capable of renewing its own democratic compacts while fighting for its values abroad. While America has not always lived up to its ideals, the truth remains that many people around the world still look to American democracy for inspiration and support. This unique role can and must outlast President Trump. America's future security and prosperity will in turn depend in large part on whether the United States can continue to defend and lead the world's democratic community. To prevail over the current illiberal challenge and preserve its place as the world's leading nation, America needs to revive and harness the power of democratic values.

Notes

1. Landon R. Y. Storrs, "The Ugly History Behind Trump's
   Attacks on Civil Servants," *Politico Magazine*, March 26, 2017,
   available at https://www.politico.com/magazine
   /story/2017/03/history-trump-attacks-civil-service-federal
   -workers-mccarthy-214951; Brennan Center for Justice, "In
   His Own Words: The President's Attacks on the Courts," June
   5, 2017, available at https://www.brennancenter.org
   /analysis/his-own-words-presidents-attacks-courts; Philip
   Rucker, "Trump rails against Mueller investigation, dismisses
   McCabe's notes as 'Fake Memos,'" *The Washington Post*, March
   18, 2018, available at https://www.washingtonpost.com
   /politics/trump-rails-against-mueller-investigation-dismisses
   -mccabes-notes-as-fake-memos/2018/03/18/30e71546-2aaa
   -11e8-b0b0-f706877db618_story.html; Kurt Bardella, "With
   Trump on the attack, Congress must defend free press," CNN,
   April 6, 2018, available at https://www.cnn.com/2018/04/06
   /opinions/congress-prioritize-protecting-journalists-bardella
   -opinion/index.html.

2. See data from 1970 to 2010 from Center for Systemic Peace,
   "The Polity Project," available at http://www.systemicpeace
   .org/polityproject.html (last accessed August 2018); Pew
   Research Center, "Nearly six-in-ten governments are
   democracies," December 4, 2017, available at http://www
   .pewresearch.org/fact-tank/2017/12/06/despite-concerns
   -about-global-democracy-nearly-six-in-ten-countries-are
   -now-democratic/ft_17-11-10_demo_auto_trend/.

3. Max Roser, "Democracy," OurWorldinData.org (2018), available
   at https://ourworldindata.org/democracy.

4. Steven Pinker, "Has the Decline of Violence Reversed since the
   Better Angels of Our Nature Was Written?" (Cambridge, MA:
   Harvard University, 2014), available at https://stevenpinker
   .com/files/pinker/files/has_the_decline_of_violence_
   reversed_since_the_better_angels_of_our_nature_was_
   written_2017.pdf.

5. Banu Eligür, "Turkey's Declining Democracy," Hudson Institute,
   July 22, 2014, available at https://www.hudson.org
   /research/10525-turkey-s-declining-democracy; Christian
   Davies, "Hostile Takeover: How Law and Justice Captured

Poland's Courts" (Washington: Freedom House, 2018),
available at https://freedomhouse.org/report/special-reports
/hostile-takeover-how-law-and-justice-captured-poland-s
-courts; Valeriya Mechkova, Anna Lührmann, and Staffan I.
Lindberg, "How Much Democratic Backsliding?" *Journal of
Democracy* 28 (4) (2017): 162–169, available at http://muse
.jhu.edu/article/671998.

6. William A. Galston, "The rise of European populism and the
collapse of the center-left," Brookings Institution, March 8,
2018, available at https://www.brookings.edu
/blog/order-from-chaos/2018/03/08/the-rise-of-european
-populism-and-the-collapse-of-the-center-left/; Matt Browne,
Dalibor Rohac, and Carolyn Kenney, "Europe's Populist
Challenge: Origins, Supporters, and Responses" (Washington:
Center for American Progress, 2018), available at https://
americanprogress.org/issues/democracy
/reports/2018/05/10/450430/europes-populist-challenge/.

7. Soner Cagaptay and Oya Rose Aktas, "How Erdoganism Is
Killing Turkish Democracy," *Foreign Affairs*, July 7, 2017,
available at https://www.foreignaffairs.com/articles
/turkey/2017-07-07/how-erdoganism-killing-turkish
-democracy.

8. Jan-Werner Müller, "Homo Orbánicus," *The New York Review of
Books*, April 5, 2018, available at http://www.nybooks.com
/articles/2018/04/05/homo-orbanicus-hungary/.

9. Adam J. Chmeilewski, "Unsympathetic people: the
overwhelming success of Poland's exclusionary agenda,"
openDemocracy, April 23, 2018, available at https://www
.opendemocracy.net/can-europe-make-it/adam-chmielewski
/unsympathetic-people-and-overwhelming-success-of
-polands-exclusi.

10. Human Rights Watch, "Philippines: Events of 2017" (2018)
available at https://www.hrw.org/world-report/2018/country
-chapters/philippines.

11. Christopher de Bellaigue, "Welcome to demokrasi: how
Erdoğan got more popular than ever," *The Guardian*, August
30, 2016, available at https://www.theguardian
.com/world/2016/aug/30/welcome-to-demokrasi-how
-erdogan-got-more-popular-than-ever; Portfolio, "Approval

rating of Hungary's ruling Fidesz party at 7-year high,"
February 9, 2018, available at http://www.portfolio.hu/en
/economy/approval-rating-of-hungarys-ruling-fidesz-party
-at-7-year-high.35469.html; Aleks Szczerbiak, "Explaining the
popularity of Poland's Law and Justice government," EUROPP,
October 26, 2017, available at http://blogs.lse
.ac.uk/europpblog/2017/10/26/explaining-the-popularity
-of-polands-law-and-justice-government/; Reuters, "Survey
shows Filipinos more satisfied with Duterte government than
any other," January 18, 2018, available at https://www.reuters
.com/article/us-philippines-duterte/survey-shows-filipinos
-more-satisfied-with-duterte-government-than-any-other
-idUSKBN1F70XA.

12. Veronica Stracqualursi and Kevin Liptak, "Trump says he
wants 'my people' to 'sit up at attention' like North Koreans,
later says he's 'kidding,'" CNN, June 15, 2018, available at
https://www.cnn.com/2018/06/15/politics/trump-north
-korea-kim-jong-un/index.html.

13. Daniel Eizenga and Leonardo A. Villalon, "Taking stock
of Burkina Faso's democracy after al-Qaeda attack," *The
Washington Post*, January 21, 2016, available at https://www
.washingtonpost.com/news/monkey-cage/wp/2016/01/21
/taking-stock-of-burkina-fasos-democracy-after-al-qaeda
-attack/; Rayhan Demytrie, "Why Armenia 'Velvet Revolution'
won without a bullet fired," BBC News, May 1, 2018, available
at https://www.bbc.com/news/world-europe-43948181;
Josh Rogin, "In Malaysia, a victory for democracy—and an
opportunity for the U.S.," *The Washington Post*, June 7, 2018,
available at https://www.washingtonpost.com/opinions
/global-opinions/in-malaysia-a-victory-for-democracy–and
-an-opportunity-for-the-us/2018/06/07/b365a928-6a8e-11e8
-bea7-c8eb28bc52b1_story.html?utm_term=.50c9518ed2cc.

14. Adam Bonica and others, "Why Hasn't Democracy Slowed
Rising Inequality?" *Journal of Economic Perspectives* 27 (3)
(2013): 103–124, available at https://pubs.aeaweb.org
/doi/pdfplus/10.1257/jep.27.3.103; Karen Rowlingson, "Does
income inequality cause health and social problems" (York,
U.K.: Joseph Rowntree Foundation, 2011), available at https://
www.jrf.org.uk/sites/default/files/jrf/migrated/files/inequality
-income-social-problems-full.pdf.

15. Richard Wike and others, "Globally, Broad Support for Representative and Direct Democracy" (Washington: Pew Research Center, 2017), available at http://www.pewglobal.org/2017/10/16/many-unhappy-with-current-political-system/.

16. Ronald F. Inglehart and Pippa Norris, "Trump, Brexit and the Rise of Populism: Economic Have-Nots and Cultural Backlash" (Cambridge: Harvard Kennedy School, 2016), available at https://research.hks.harvard.edu/publications/getFile.aspx?Id=1401; Pippa Norris, "It's not just Trump. Authoritarian populism is rising across the West. Here's why." *The Washington Post*, March 11, 2016, available at https://www.washingtonpost.com/news/monkey-cage/wp/2016/03/11/its-not-just-trump-authoritarian-populism-is-rising-across-the-west-heres-why/.

17. Pew Research Center, "Public Trust in Government: 1958-2017," December 14, 2017, available at http://www.people-press.org/2017/12/14/public-trust-in-government-1958-2017/; The Democracy Project, "Reversing a Crisis of Confidence" (2018), available at https://www.democracyprojectreport.org/report.

18. Dalibor Rohac, Liz Kennedy, and Vikram Singh, "Drivers of Authoritarian Populism in the United States: A Primer" (Washington: Center for American Progress, 2018), available at https://americanprogress.org/issues/democracy/reports/2018/05/10/450552/drivers-authoritarian-populism-united-states/.

19. Alexander Cooley, "Whose Rules, Whose Sphere? Russian Governance and Influence in Post-Soviet States" (Washington: Carnegie Endowment for International Peace, 2017), available at http://carnegieendowment.org/2017/06/30/whose-rules-whose-sphere-russian-governance-and-influence-in-post-soviet-states-pub-71403; Mark Galeotti, "Controlling Chaos: How Russia manages its political war in Europe" (London: European Council on Foreign Relations, 2017), available at http://www.ecfr.eu/publications/summary/controlling_chaos_how_russia_manages_its_political_war_in_europe.

20. Max Bergmann and Carolyn Kenney, "Acts of an Adversary: Russia's Ongoing Hostilities Toward the United States and Its

Allies" (Washington: Center for American Progress, 2017), available at https://americanprogress.org/issues /security/reports/2017/12/05/443574/acts-of-an-adversary/; Max Bergmann and Carolyn Kenney, "War by Other Means: Russian Active Measures and Weaponization of Information" (Washington: Center for American Progress, 2017), available at https://americanprogress.org/issues/security /reports/2017/06/06/433345/war-by-other-means/.

21. Warren Strobel and John Walcott, "Russia ran U.S. election interference, no Trump collusion: panel Republicans," Reuters, April 27, 2018, available at https://www.reuters .com/article/us-usa-trump-russia-house/russia-ran-u-s -election-interference-no-trump-collusion-panel-republicans -idUSKBN1HY1X4.

22. He Li, "The Chinese Model of Development and Its Implications," *World Journal of Social Science Research* (2) (2015): 128-138, available at https://scholarworks.merrimack .edu/cgi/viewcontent.cgi?article=1017&context=pol_facpub; Seth D. Kaplan, "Development with Chinese Characteristics," The American Interest, January 3, 2018, available at https:// www.the-american-interest.com/2018/01/03/development -chinese-characteristics/.

23. Abraham Denmark, "A New Era of Intensified U.S.-China Competition," Asia Dispatches, January 4, 2018, available at https://www.wilsoncenter.org/blog-post/new-era-intensified -us-china-competition.

24. Eric B. Lorber, "Economic Coercion, with a Chinese Twist," *Foreign Policy*, February 28, 2017, available at http:// foreignpolicy.com/2017/02/28/economic-coercion-china -united-states-sanctions-asia/.

25. Tom Phillips, Oliver Holmes, and Owen Bowcott, "Beijing rejects tribunal's ruling in South China Sea case," *The Guardian*, July 12, 2016, available at https://www.theguardian .com/world/2016/jul/12/philippines-wins-south-china-sea -case-against-china.

26. Rodrigo Campos, "Human rights chief slams Security Council for inaction on Syria," Reuters, March 20, 2018, available at https://www.reuters.com/article/us-mideast-crisis-un-syria

/human-rights-chief-slams-security-council-for-inaction-on
-syria-idUSKBN1GW005.

27. Jacob M. Schlesinger, "How China Swallowed the WTO," *The
Wall Street Journal*, November 1, 2017, available at https://
www.wsj.com/articles/how-china-swallowed-the
-wto-1509551308.

28. Catharin E. Dalpino, "Does Globalization Promote
Democracy? An early assessment," Brookings, September 1,
2001, available at https://www.brookings.edu/articles/does
-globalization-promote-democracy-an-early-assessment/.

29. Alex Cooley and Jason Sharman, "How today's despots and
kleptocrats hide their stolen wealth," *The Washington Post*,
November 14, 2017, available at https://www.washingtonpost
.com/news/monkey-cage/wp/2017/11/14/theres-a-dirty
-little-secret-behind-western-condescension-toward-foreign
-kleptocrats/?utm_term=.0c6351503e8a.

30. Alexander Cooley, John Heathershaw, and J. C. Sharman,
"The Rise of Kleptocracy: Laundering Cash, Whitewashing
Reputations," *Journal of Democracy* 29 (1) (2018): 29–43,
available at https://www.journalofdemocracy.org/article/rise
-kleptocracy-laundering-cash-whitewashing-reputations.

31. Joseph Spanjers and Håkon Frede Foss, "Illicit Financial Flows
and Development Indices: 2008–2012" (Washington: Global
Financial Integrity, 2015), available at http://www.gfintegrity
.org/wp-content/uploads/2015/05/Illicit-Financial-Flows-and
-Development-Indices-2008-2012.pdf.

32. Conor Finnegan, "Tillerson: Pushing human rights abroad
'creates obstacles' to US interests," ABC News, May 3, 2017,
available at https://abcnews.go.com/Politics/tillerson-pushing
-human-rights-abroad-creates-obstacles/story?id=47190743.

33. Kelly Magsamen and Michael Fuchs, "Destroying the
Foundations of U.S. Foreign Policy" (Washington:
Center for American Progress, 2018), available at https://
americanprogress.org/issues/security/reports/2018/06/28
/452913/destroying-foundations-u-s-foreign-policy/.

34. As the German minister of foreign affairs, Heiko Maas,
explained in a speech after the G-7 summit, "Old pillars of
reliability are crumbling under the weight of new crises and
alliances dating back decades are being challenged in the time

it takes to write a tweet. The US was long the leading power among the free nations. For 70 years, it was committed to freedom, prosperity and security here in Europe. … However, the Atlantic has become wider under President Trump and his policy of isolationism has left a giant vacuum around the world." See Federal Foreign Office, "Speech by Foreign Minister Heiko Maas: Courage to Stand Up for Europe— #EuropeUnited," June 13, 2018, available at https://www .auswaertiges-amt.de/en/newsroom/news/maas -europeunited/2106528.

35. Sean M. Lynn-Jones, "Why the United States Should Spread Democracy" (Cambridge, MA: Belfer Center for Science and International Affairs, 1998), available at https://www .belfercenter.org/publication/why-united-states-should -spread-democracy.

36. Morton H. Halperin, Joseph T. Siegle, and Michael M. Weinstein, The Democracy Advantage (New York: Routledge, 2004).

37. V-Dem Institute, "V-Dem Annual Democracy Report 2018. Democracy for All?" (2018), available at https://www.v-dem .net/media/filer_public/68/51/685150f0-47e1-4d03-97bc -45609c3f158d/v-dem_annual_dem_report_2018.pdf; Center for Systemic Peace, "The Polity Project," available at http:// www.systemicpeace.org/polityproject.html (last accessed August 2018).

38. Coral Davenport, "How Much Has 'Climate Change' Been Scrubbed From Federal Websites? A Lot." *The New York Times,* January 10, 2018, available at https://www.nytimes .com/2018/01/10/climate/climate-change-trump.html.

39. Although recommendations for addressing these domestic challenges are beyond the scope of this paper, CAP has produced a wide range of relevant policy analysis on these topics. See, for example, Center for American Progress, "Blueprint for the 21st Century" (2018), available at https:// americanprogress.org/issues/economy/reports/2018 /05/14/450856/blueprint-21st-century/; CAP Health Policy Team "Medicare Extra for All: A Plan to Guarantee Universal Health Coverage in the United States" (Washington: Center for American Progress, 2018), available at https://

americanprogress.org/issues/healthcare/reports/2018/02/22/447095/medicare-extra-for-all/; Angela Hanks, Danyelle Solomon, and Christian E. Weller, "Systematic Inequality: How America's Structural Racism Helped Create the Black-White Wealth Gap" (Washington: Center for American Progress, 2018), available at https://americanprogress.org/issues/race/reports/2018/02/21/447051/systematic-inequality/; Center for American Progress, "6 Ways to Reduce Gun Violence in America" (2018), available at https://americanprogress.org/issues/guns-crime/news/2018/03/28/448565/gun-violence-united-states-public-health-crisis/; Neil Davey, "Congress Must Do More to Address the U.S. Opioid Epidemic," Center for American Progress, August 25, 2016, available at https://americanprogress.org/issues/healthcare/news/2016/08/25/143020/congress-must-do-more-to-address-the-u-s-opioid-epidemic/; Center for American Progress, "Bold Ideas for State Action" (2018), available at https://americanprogress.org/issues/general/reports/2018/05/10/450580/bold-ideas-state-action/.

40. Max Bergmann and Carolyn Kenney, "War by Other Means," (Washington: Center for American Progress, June 2017), available at https://americanprogress.org/issues/security/reports/2017/06/06/433345/war-by-other-means/; Gisela Grieger, "China's foreign influence operations in Western liberal democracies: An emerging debate," (Brussels: European Parliamentary Research Service, May 2018), available at http://www.europarl.europa.eu/RegData/etudes/ATAG/2018/621875/EPRS_ATA(2018)621875_EN.pdf.

41. These vulnerabilities and some potential approaches to addressing them were examined in the following reports: Bergmann and Kenney, "War by Other Means"; Diana Pilipenko, "Cracking the Shell: Trump and the Corrupting Potential of Furtive Russian Money" (Washington: Center for American Progress, 2018), available at https://americanprogress.org/issues/democracy/reports/2018/02/13/446576/cracking-the-shell/; Jamie Fly, Laura Rosenberger, and David Salvo, "The ASD Policy Blueprint for Countering Authoritarian Interference in Democracies" (Washington: German Marshall Fund, 2018),

available at http://www.gmfus.org/publications/asd-policy-blueprint-countering-authoritarian-interference-democracies.

42. Liz Sidoti, "McCain Favors a 'League of Democracies,'" *The Washington Post*, April 30, 2007, available at http://www.washingtonpost.com/wp-dyn/content/article/2007/04/30/AR2007043001402.html.

43. Anna Ohanyan, "What's next for Armenia's protest movement?" Al Jazeera, May 1, 2018, available at https://www.aljazeera.com/indepth/opinion/armenia-protest-movement-180501091308469.html; BBC, "Slovakia protests: 65,000 join Bratislava anti-government protests," March 16, 2018, available at https://www.bbc.com/news/world-europe-43437993.

Organizations to Contact

The editors have compiled the following list of organizations concerned with the issues debated in this book. The descriptions are derived from materials provided by the organizations. All have publications or information available for interested readers. This list was compiled on the date of publication of the present volume; the information provided here may change. Be aware that many organizations take several weeks or longer to respond to inquiries, so allow as much time as possible.

American Enterprise Institute

1789 Massachusetts Avenue NW
Washington, DC 20036
(202) 862-5800
website: www.aei.org

Founded in 1943, the American Enterprise Institute (AEI) is a research and advocacy organization dedicated to promoting democracy, free enterprise, and American global leadership. AEI scholars conduct research in a wide variety of fields including economics, education, health care, and foreign policy.

Brookings Institution

1775 Massachusetts Avenue NW
Washington, DC 20036
(202) 797-6000
email: communications@brookings.edu
website: www.brookings.edu

With over 300 academic and government experts, the Brookings Institution is one of the premier policy think tanks in the United States. Brookings experts conduct research on foreign policy, economics, development and governance, and provide policy recommendations based on that research.

Center for American Progress
1333 H Street NW, 10th Floor
Washington, DC 20005
(202) 682-1611
website: www.americanprogress.org

The Center for American Progress (CAP) is a liberal-leaning think tank focused on economic issues in the United States, including income inequality, tax policy, and education. With an extensive communications and outreach infrastructure, CAP works to ensure that progressive ideals are represented in the national political conversation.

Democratic National Committee
430 South Capitol Street SE
Washington, DC 20003
(202) 863-8000
website: www.democrats.org

Since 1848, the Democratic National Committee has been the home of the Democratic Party, the oldest continuing party in the United States.

National Democratic Institute
455 Massachusetts Avenue NW, 8th Floor
Washington, DC 20001-2621
(202) 728-5500
website: www.ndi.org

The National Democratic Institute is a nonprofit, nonpartisan, nongovernmental organization that has supported democratic institutions and practices in every region of the world for more than three decades. Since its founding in 1983, NDI and its local partners have worked to establish and strengthen political and civic organizations, safeguard elections, and promote citizen participation, openness, and accountability in government.

Peterson Institute for International Economics
1750 Massachusetts Avenue NW
Washington, DC 20036
(202) 328-9000
email: comments@piie.com
website: www.piie.com

The Peterson Institute for International Economics (PIIE) is a private, nonpartisan think tank dedicated to the study of economics, trade policy, and globalization. PIIE conducts research on emerging issues, develops policy ideas, and works to educate government officials, business leaders, and the public on international economic issues.

Republican National Committee
310 First Street SE
Washington, DC 20003
(202) 863-8500
website: www.gop.com

The Republican National Committee is a US political committee that provides national leadership for the Republican Party of the United States.

United Nations
760 United Nations Plaza
New York, NY 10017
(212) 963-4475
email: education-outreach@un.org
website: www.un.org

Currently made up of 193 member states, the UN is guided by the purposes and principles contained in its founding charter. It is the preeminent venue for nations from around the world to gather, discuss common problems, and find shared solutions that benefit all of humanity.

United States Department of Defense
Office of the Secretary
The Pentagon
Washington, DC 20301
(703) 545-6700
website: www.defense.gov

The United States Department of Defense is America's largest government agency. Its mission is to provide the country with the military forces needed to deter war and ensure the nation's security.

United States Department of Homeland Security
2707 Martin Luther King Jr. Avenue SE
Washington, DC 20528
(202) 282-8000
website: www.dhs.gov

The Department of Homeland Security works to secure the United States from the many threats it faces. This requires the dedication of more than 240,000 employees in jobs that range from aviation and border security to emergency response, from cybersecurity analyst to chemical facility inspector.

United States Department of State
Harry S. Truman Building
2201 C Street NW
Washington, DC 20240
(202) 208-3100
website: www.state.gov

The United States Department of State leads America's foreign policy through diplomacy, advocacy, and assistance by advancing the interests of the American people, their safety, and economic prosperity.

World Economic Forum
350 Madison Avenue, 11th Floor
New York, NY 10017
(212) 703-2300
email: forumusa@weforum.org
website: www.weforum.org

The World Economic Forum is a nonprofit organization based in Geneva. It is focused on facilitating public-private cooperation and policy agreement in the interest of promoting a healthy, stable global economic environment.

Bibliography

Books

Spencer Ackerman. *Reign of Terror: How the 9/11 Era Destabilized America and Produced Trump.* New York, NY: Viking, 2021.

Anne Applebaum. *Twilight of Democracy: The Seductive Lure of Authoritarianism.* New York, NY: Anchor Books, 2020.

Daniel P. Bolger. *Why We Lost: A General's Inside Account of the Iraq and Afghanistan Wars.* New York, NY: Houghton Mifflin Harcourt, 2015.

Ray Dalio. *Principles for Dealing with the Changing World Order: Why Nations Succeed and Fail.* New York, NY: Avid Reader Press, 2021.

Ryan Hass. *Stronger: Adapting America's China Strategy in an Age of Competitive Interdependence.* New Haven, CT: Yale University Press, 2021.

William E. Hudson. *American Democracy in Peril: Eight Challenges to America's Future.* Thousand Oaks, CA: SAGE Publications, Inc., 2021.

Oscar Jonsson. *The Russian Understanding of War: Blurring the Lines Between War and Peace.* Washington, DC: Georgetown University Press, 2019.

Rebekah Koffler. *Putin's Playbook: Russia's Secret Plan to Defeat America.* Washington, DC: Regnery Gateway, 2021.

Herbert Lin and Amy Zegart, eds. *Bytes, Bombs, and Spies: The Strategic Dimensions of Offensive Cyber Operations.* Washington, DC: The Brookings Institution, 2018.

Kishore Mahbubani. *Has China Won? The Chinese Challenge to American Primacy.* New York, NY: Public Affairs, 2020.

Mitchell A. Orenstein. *The Lands in Between: Russia vs. the West and the New Politics of Hybrid War.* New York, NY: Oxford University Press, 2019.

Clyde Prestowitz. *The World Turned Upside Down: America, China, and the Struggle for Global Leadership.* New Haven, CT: Yale University Press, 2021.

David E. Sanger. *The Perfect Weapon: War, Sabotage, and Fear in the Cyber Age.* New York, NY: Broadway Books, 2018.

Joseph E. Stiglitz. *Globalization and Its Discontents Revisited: Anti-Globalization in the Era of Trump.* New York, NY: W. W. Norton & Company, 2018.

Craig Whitlock. *The Afghanistan Papers: A Secret History of the War.* New York, NY: Simon & Schuster, 2021.

Periodicals and Internet Sources

Michael Beckley and Hal Brands, "What Will Drive China to War?" *The Atlantic*, November 1, 2021. https://www.theatlantic.com/ideas/archive/2021/11/us-china-war/620571/.

Marwan Bishara, "China's Rise and America's Decline Spell Conflict," Al Jazeera, November 21, 2021. https://www.aljazeera.com/opinions/2021/11/18/the-chinese-miracle-and-the-american-debacle.

John R. Deni, "NATO Must Adapt to an Era of Hybrid Threats," Carnegie Europe, December 2, 2021. https://carnegieeurope.eu/strategiceurope/85900.

Farhad Manjoo, "The Year America Lost Its Democracy," *New York Times*, December 8, 2021. https://www.nytimes.com/2021/12/08/opinion/american-democracy.html.

Alfred McCoy, "America's Decline Started at Home," *The Nation*, November 22, 2021. https://www.thenation.com/article/world/american-hegemony-climate.

Tom McTague, "The Decline of the American World," *The Atlantic*, June 24, 2020. https://www.theatlantic.com/international/archive/2020/06/america-image-power-trump/613228/.

William Moloney, "American Decline: Perception or Reality," *The Hill*, April 5, 2021. https://thehill.com/opinion/finance/546209-american-decline-perception-or-reality.

Michael Schuman, "China Wants to Rule the World by Controlling the Rules," *The Atlantic*, December 9, 2021. https://www.theatlantic.com/international/archive/2021/12/china-wants-rule-world-controlling-rules/620890/.

Michael D. Shear and Jim Tankersley, "Biden Defends Afghan Pullout and Declares an End to Nation-Building," *New York Times*, August 31, 2021. https://www.nytimes.com/2021/08/31/us/politics/biden-defends-afghanistan-withdrawal.html.

Justin Sherman, "How to Regulate the Internet Without Becoming a Dictator," *Foreign Policy*, February 18, 2019. https://foreignpolicy.com/2019/02/18/how-to-regulate-the-internet-without-becoming-a-dictator-uk-britain-cybersecurity-china-russia-data-content-filtering/.

Raymond Zhong, "Taiwan, Trade, Tech, and More: A Tense Era in U.S.-China Ties," *New York Times*, November 17, 2021. https://www.nytimes.com/article/us-china-tensions-explained.html.

Index